STACEY THE MATH WHIZ

**Other books by
Ann M. Martin**

STACEY THE MATH WHIZ

Ann M. Martin

AN
APPLE
PAPERBACK

SCHOLASTIC INC.
New York Toronto London Auckland Sydney

This book is in memory of Jessica Knott,
and in honor of Liesl Flandermeyer
and all of Jessica's friends.

Many thanks to Peter G. Hayes

The author gratefully acknowledges
Peter Lerangis
for his help in
preparing this manuscript.

Cover art by Hodges Soileau

ISBN 0-590-69211-9

12 11 10 9 8 7 6 5 4 3 2 1   7 8 9/9 0 1/0

Printed in the U.S.A.   40

First Scholastic printing, February 1997

CHAPTER 1

*R*RRRRIIINNNNNG!

"Yeaaa!"

"All riiiiight!"

"Yyyyyyyes!"

Around me, kids shouted with joy and relief. They stood up at once, laughing and talking. Can you tell where I was?

The start of the circus? Halftime at a Stoneybrook Middle School football game?

No. The end of math class. Which also happens to be the end of the school day.

Math and *last period* are two concepts that don't mix very well. Most of my classmates come in looking as if they're ready for a nap. They leave as if they've been released from prison.

Me? I don't mind math class. In fact, I think it's interesting and fun. I wish my teacher, Mr. Zizmore, would go a little faster. What I don't like is sitting around while he repeats things seventeen times for the class sleepyheads.

Which is why I'd spent the last fifteen minutes writing an original book on looseleaf sheets hidden inside my textbook. It's called *The Stacey McGill Guide to Third-Grade Math*. (Actually, I'm in eighth grade, but I happened to be tutoring an eight-year-old girl named Lindsey DeWitt.)

I slapped my textbook shut and stood up from my seat. Kids were chatting away. Mr. Zizmore was examining a note on a small pink slip.

"Stacey?" he called out. "Ms. Hartley would like to see you in Room two-oh-eight after school."

Ms. Hartley is the chairperson of the Stoneybrook Middle School math department. Why did she want to see me? I had no idea.

"Ooooooh, bad girl . . ." murmured Irv Hirsch, the Stupid-Prank King of SMS, who just happens to sit behind me.

I ignored him. As I lifted the books off my desk, a sheet of my work-in-progress fell out. I tried to grab it, but Irv beat me to it.

"Attention, ladies and gentlemen," he said with a mock-English accent, "the notes of the class genius! I quote: 'Subtraction of three-digit numbers, those with numeral values in the hundreds, tens, and ones columns, must be arranged with the subtrahend below the minuend and answered from right to left.' Whoa, when did we learn this?"

I snatched the sheet away. "In third grade. Maybe you were absent that day."

"What's a *minuend*?"

I did not answer him. I marched out of the room and down the hall.

What a dork.

"Dode say hi or eddythigg," called a familiar stuffed-up voice.

I turned to see Abby Stevenson walking toward me, loaded down with books. "Sorry," I said. "I was too busy being mad at Irv."

"Dode get bad, get evedd," Abby said. "That's by botto." (No, Abby didn't have a cold. She's allergic to just about anything you can think of — dust, pollen, shellfish, strawberries, dog fur, you name it.)

"How?"

"He's id by sciedce class. I could put a dissected frog in his backpack."

I cracked up. It wasn't a bad idea.

Leave it to Abby. She's the best remedy for a bad mood. Everything about her is funny. Take her hair. It's this thick brown curly mop. On that day, she'd decided to gather it on the top of her head. It looked like an exploding volcano.

I don't mean to make fun of her. Just the opposite. Here's the Stacey McGill Philosophy of

3

Appearance, Rule One: If you feel confident on the inside, you look great on the outside, no matter what you wear. Abby doesn't care what people think about her appearance. I admire that.

Rule Number Two? If you can't be confident all the time, wear cool clothes. That's the rule I obey. For me, the hardest part of the day is deciding what to wear in the morning. My mom has to hide our mail-order catalogs if she hopes to get a glimpse of them. Fashion is my passion. I can't help it. I like nice clothes the way some people like chocolate.

Actually, I can't even eat chocolate. I have this condition called diabetes. You've heard of sugar shock? Well, diabetes is a mega-case of that. My body can't store sugar and parcel it into my bloodstream a bit at a time, the way it's supposed to. Instead — wham! — the sugar goes right into the bloodstream. If I eat too much sugar, I could have serious problems, even pass out. But don't worry. Life without sweets is fine. To me, it's normal. As long as I eat meals on a strict schedule and give myself daily injections of a hormone called insulin (which is not as gross as it sounds), I lead a pretty normal life.

While we're on the subject, here are some other things you need to know about me: I'm thirteen years old. I have long, golden-blonde hair. I grew up in New York City. My parents are divorced.

My parents were not divorced when we first moved to Stoneybrook, Connecticut. My dad's company had transferred him here from the Big Apple. It was hard to adjust to the suburbs, but I did — until Dad was transferred back. Zoom, off to the city again. I felt like a Ping-Pong ball. Then my parents' marriage fell apart, and I had a choice: stay with Dad in New York or move with Mom to Stoneybrook.

I, Stacey the City Girl, who can draw a map of the NYC subway system from memory, who wore out the sidewalks in front of my neighborhood boutiques, decided on Stoneybrook. Why? Three words. The Baby-sitters Club. (Or is that four words? Whatever. It's a group of best friends, which I'll tell you about later.)

Abby's a member of our group. She's also a New Yorker. Actually, a Long Islander, which is different than a Manhattanite, but I won't bore you with the details.

"Walk with be to by locker?" Abby asked.

"Not today," I replied. "I'm supposed to see Ms. Hartley after school."

"Is she givig you sub kide of bath award?"

I shrugged. (Bath award? For some reason, all I could think about was a bronze statuette in the shape of a rubber duckie.)

At the corner of the hallway, we said good-bye and I walked to Room 208. Ms. Hartley looked up from her desk and smiled. "Hello, Stacey! Would you mind closing the door? I'd like to continue a discussion we began in September."

Huh? As I shut the door, I searched through my memory.

"It's been a fantastic year for Mathletes," Ms. Hartley continued, "as I'm sure you've heard."

Ugh. Now I remembered. Ms. Hartley had asked me if I wanted to join this after-school group called Mathletes. It's sort of like a sports team, with practices and meets. Only instead of hitting home runs or kicking a ball, you solve tricky math problems.

I know. You're falling off your chair with excitement. You're slapping your forehead and thinking, how could I possibly say no to such a fabulous offer?

Just kidding.

Puh-leeze. Like I had nothing better to do than hang out with math geeks on permanent Bad Hair Days?

"It's a special team this year, Stacey," Ms. Hartley went on. "We have tons of fun at our practices. But more to the point, for the first time in Stoneybrook history, I believe we have the chance to go all the way this year. To the state championships. *That's* how much potential this team has."

All I could manage was a not-too-enthusiastic "wow."

"Unfortunately, one of our star members has moved to Ohio. Now, I know I've asked you before, Stacey, but I'd like you to reconsider joining. Mr. Zizmore has shown me some of your excellent work, and he says you have a real passion for the material. I think you and the Mathletes would be a perfect match."

"Ms. Hartley," I began, "I've been really busy with baby-sitting and homework and — "

"The season only has a month to go," Ms. Hartley interrupted. "This weekend we start competing at the local level, but you wouldn't have to start then if you felt unprepared. Most of our meets are on weekends, but the state finals are a best-of-three series, and I think some of it occurs during the week. Our practices are informal. Sometimes we meet here in this room after school, sometimes at a student's house or my own. We eat snacks, tell jokes . . . it's like a big party, only we solve interesting math problems. Stacey, with a mind like yours, we would be honored to have you as a member."

I laughed. "I'm not *that* good."

"Oh?" Ms. Hartley leaned toward me and lowered her voice. "Well, let me settle your doubts. I'm not at liberty to tell you the exact numbers, but I can say your standardized test scores are among the highest we've ever seen in this district."

Whoa. Highest ever? Me?

I felt kind of flushed. Almost embarrassed. "I didn't know that."

"Not that I'm trying to pressure you," Ms. Hartley continued. "I'd just like you to consider it. Our next practice is Friday at seven-thirty at my house, Four-seven-seven Komorn Road. Come and hang out with us."

"Maybe," I said with a shrug.

Ms. Hartley's face brightened. She rose from her seat and extended her hand. "Hope to see you, Stacey."

"Uh-huh," I said, shaking her hand. " 'Bye."

I felt kind of weird as I left. Me, a Mathlete? The idea seemed ridiculous. I pictured myself in high-water pants, my pockets stuffed with calculators and my head in the clouds.

Don't be such a snob, part of me was saying. It might be fun.

Besides, if my aptitude was so high, I should make the most of it. Being on a state championship team would be cool.

I held that thought for about a minute. Then it flew out, like the air from a balloon.

I ran to my locker. I had to go home, to begin preparing dinner so my mom wouldn't have to do it all when she returned from work. Then I had to go to a Baby-sitters Club meeting.

Mathletes shmathletes. Maybe in another life. This one was complicated enough.

CHAPTER 2

"So, my teacher's handing back my social studies test, and I can see this big red word written across the top," Claudia Kishi said, emerging from her closet. In her right hand was a bag of Cheez Doodles, in her left a box of peanut M&M's. "Healthy or nonhealthy?"

"That's three words," said Kristy Thomas.

"I'm asking which snack you want!" Claudia retorted.

"Which one are you calling healthy?" Jessi Ramsey asked.

"This has cheese," Claudia said, holding out the Doodles. "Actually, the M&M's have peanuts, so I guess they both qualify."

"Claudia Kishi, nutrition expert," Abby remarked.

"What did your teacher write on your test?" Mary Anne Spier asked.

Claudia passed around both bags. "Well, I

figured it was, 'Try harder,' or 'See me,' or 'You must be joking.' So I closed my eyes. But when she put it on my desk, I peeked and saw . . . 'Excellent' with a big explanation mark. I nearly had a heart attack! I figured it was some mistake."

"Excla*mation*," Mallory Pike corrected her.

"Whatever. Anyway, I think I'm going to frame it."

Kristy was shoving a handful of M&M's into her mouth as Claudia's clock clicked to 5:30. "I hooby call zuff meetee to order," she mumbled.

Abby rolled her eyes. "Very high class, Kristy."

Welcome to our Wednesday Baby-sitters Club meeting. We were in Claudia's bedroom, engaging in our favorite activity, pigging out. (I, Stacey the Sugar-Free, was noshing on some Ruffles Claudia had pulled from behind her night table.)

Claudia hoards junk food. She also has her own private phone. Those are the two reasons we use her room as our headquarters. We meet every Monday, Wednesday, and Friday, from five-thirty to six. During that time, Stoneybrook parents phone us to line up baby-sitting jobs. With one call, they can contact seven reliable, experienced baby-sitters.

Our clients love the convenience. We love the business. Our charges look forward to seeing us.

Who thought of this brilliant idea? Our president, founder, and expert on bad food manners, Kristy Thomas.

The idea came to her one evening, back when Kristy lived across the street from Claudia. Mrs. Thomas needed a sitter for Kristy's little brother, David Michael. Usually Kristy and her two older brothers baby-sat, but they were busy. (Mr. Thomas, by the way, was out of the picture; he'd abandoned the family shortly after David Michael was born.) Well, Mrs. Thomas was on the phone for hours but she couldn't find one available sitter.

Sha-zam! The idea for the BSC began forming in Kristy's brain.

We started with four members: Kristy, Claudia, Mary Anne Spier, and me. But parents began knocking down our doors, tying up the phone lines, breaking into fights over appointments. Well, not quite, but we became busy enough to grow to seven full members. Ten, if you include our two associates and one honorary member.

How do we handle all the popularity? Organization. (That's Kristy's favorite word, after "Order!") Kristy set up the club like a company, with rules, officers, and a budget. We have to write about each job in a special notebook, so we can always be aware of our clients' changing needs.

At the top of the BSC totem pole, naturally, is President Kristy. She runs our meetings and constantly dreams up new ideas. Kids and publicity are her top priorities. She organizes holiday parties, athletic competitions, and other activities for our charges. Kristy also formed a kids' softball team called Kristy's Krushers, and she thought up the Kid-Kits (boxes of toys, games, and other user-friendly stuff) that we sometimes bring along to our jobs.

Four words to describe Kristy: loud, short, rich, and casual. Very casual. Oh, all right, I'll say it. She has zero fashion sense. (No offense, jeans and sweats are great, but all the time? Puh-leeze.) With her dark brown eyes and hair, she could really develop a Winona Ryder kind of look if she wanted to. She just laughs when I suggest that, though.

Too bad. She could definitely afford a makeover now and then. Her stepdad, Watson Brewer, is a millionaire. When he married Mrs. Thomas, Kristy's family moved across town into his mansion. Actually, *madhouse* might be a better name for it. In age order, here are the people who live there: Kristy's grandmother Nannie, Watson, Kristy's mom, Charlie (who's seventeen), Sam (fifteen), Kristy, David

Michael (seven), Karen (Watson's seven-year-old daughter from a previous marriage), Andrew (Karen's four-year-old brother), Emily Michelle (a two-and-a-half-year-old Vietnamese girl adopted by Kristy's mom and Watson), and about a zillion pets. A couple of the pets travel back and forth with Karen and Andrew, who live in their mom's and stepdad's house during alternate months.

Now that Kristy lives across town, she is chauffered to meetings by her brother Charlie in his rusty old jalopy called the Junk Bucket.

Abby lives near Kristy, so she also braves the ride. She became our newest member soon after moving to Stoneybrook. We tried to recruit her twin sister, Anna, too, but she turned us down because her violin studies take up all her spare time.

"Fiddling" is how Abby describes her sister's music. Honestly, you'd never believe those two are twins. Anna wears her hair short, unlike Abby's volcano (which she's grown out since a recent cut). Anna has no allergies or asthma. Abby has both and needs to carry inhalers with her at all times. Anna is shy, studious, and not interested in sports; Abby is the BSC's number one comedian-athlete. Anna has scoliosis, but Abby does not.

Personally, I love having another New Yorker in the group. Especially one like Abby, who adores NYC. Her mom commutes to the city every day to her job in a publishing house. (Mr. Stevenson died in a car accident when the twins were nine. Abby doesn't talk about him much, and we don't ask.)

Abby's our alternate officer. She steps in whenever another officer is absent.

Who are the other officers? Claudia's our vice president. She calls herself Chief Executive for Shelter, Communications, and Hunger Prevention. If a BSC meeting were launched into space, we'd be able to survive a trip to Neptune before her junk food supply ran out. She hides chocolate Kisses in her bedspread lining, pretzel bags in her closet, cookie boxes in her underwear drawer, sweets everywhere. I can't tell you how many times I've sat on her bed and flattened a candy bar.

If Claudia's parents ever found out about her secret stash, they'd have a cow. Maybe two. Boy, are they ever straitlaced. Their motto: No junk for the body, no junk for the mind. They don't even allow popular books in the house, just classic literature, so Claudia has to hide her Nancy Drew novels.

Claudia's sister, Janine, is as conservative as her parents, plus she's an academic genius. She's in high school but she takes college-level courses. Claudia was in eighth grade but was recently dropped back to seventh.

Guess which daughter often feels like the family misfit.

Claudia's real soulmate was her grandmother, Mimi, who used to live with the Kishis. English wasn't Mimi's first language (she was a Japanese immigrant), but she and Claudia understood each other deeply.

Looking at Claudia, you'd never know she was such a junk food addict. She's trim, gorgeous, and pimple-free. She has long, silkyblack hair that never seems to sit still. One day it'll be in a French braid, the next in cornrows, the next tied to one side with some crazy hairclip. Her best outfits are assembled from odds and ends she picks up at thrift shops. I don't know how she does it. I have to see clothes in a catalog or a store, preferably on a model.

Clothing coordination is just one of Claudia's artistic talents. You should see her paintings — and drawings and sculptures and homemade jewelry. She can do it all.

"Okay, anyone have any new business?" Kristy called out over the loud munching in the room.

"Stacey does," Abby piped up. "She was sent to Ms. Hartley. I want to hear all the juicy details."

"Abbyyyyy — " I said.

Rrrriinnng!

Claudia snatched up the receiver. "Hello,

Baby-sitters Club. . . . Hi, Mrs. Braddock. . . . Uh-huh. . . . Okay, I'll get back to you. 'Bye." She hung up and looked at Mary Anne. "Matt and Haley, next Thursday, after school."

Mary Anne was already leafing through the official BSC record book. "Um . . . Jessi, Kristy, and I are free."

"I'd love to do it," Jessi spoke up.

"Okay," said Claudia, picking up the phone to call back the Braddocks.

That's how we book jobs. Simple, huh? Well, not for Mary Anne. As our secretary, she has the hardest job. She's keeper of the BSC record book. She has to know who's available to baby-sit on any given day. On a master calendar she records all of our conflicts: doctor appointments, lessons, family trips, and so on. In the back of the book she keeps an updated list of client names, addresses, phone numbers, pay rates, and information about our charges — their likes and dislikes, bedtimes, and habits.

Mary Anne's the perfect person for the job. She's thorough, patient, and unflappable. (Don't you just love that word? It makes me think of a pancake stuck to a griddle.) She's also one of the quietest, sweetest people I've ever met. If you have a problem, she'll listen carefully to every word and give great advice. But bring tissues with you, because she tends to cry a lot.

Although she is painfully shy, Mary Anne is the only BSC member with a steady boyfriend (his name is Logan Bruno). She's also best friends with Kristy Thomas, of all people. They grew up next door to each other. They even look a little alike. Both are petite with dark features. (Mary Anne's hair is cut much shorter, though, and she wears preppier clothes.)

For a long time, Mary Anne had more of a Pollyanna-ish appearance. Richard, her dad, insisted she look that way, and he had the strictest rules about TV time, bedtime, and homework. He's loosened up a lot, thank goodness. Mary Anne claims he was just going overboard trying to be Super Single Parent. You see, Mary Anne's mom died when Mary Anne was a baby, and Richard hadn't remarried.

Hold that thought.

Enter Dawn Schafer, who moved to Stoneybrook with her divorced mom and younger brother, Jeff, from California. They moved into a two-hundred-year-old farmhouse, and Dawn ended up joining the BSC. Her mom had grown up in Stoneybrook, and guess who the dashing love of her life had been in high school? Yes, Richard Spier. Of course, Dawn and Mary Anne went to work getting them together, and soon Mr. Spier and Mrs. Schafer were married, and Dawn and Mary Anne became stepsisters, living happily in the old farmhouse. Well, not completely happily. Dawn became homesick and ended up moving back to California, just as her brother had done earlier. Boy, does Mary Anne miss her. We all do.

Dawn used to be our alternate officer. Now she's in a baby-sitting group in California called the We ♥ Kids Club, which doesn't believe in officers (don't ask Kristy what she thinks of *that*). So she has become our honorary member, which means she joins us whenever she visits.

The BSC's most supremely important officer is, of course, *moi,* the treasurer. I collect dues every Monday and keep them in a manila envelope. At the end of each month I contribute to Claudia's phone bill and pay Charlie Thomas gas money. If anything's left over, we buy stuff for Kid-Kits or put the money toward special events for our charges.

Jessi and Mallory are our junior officers. They're both eleven years old, two years younger than the rest of us. Neither is allowed to baby-sit at night. Ooh, are they sore about that. Fury at their parents' rules is one of the many things that cements their friendship. They're convinced that the oldest child in the family has it the hardest. Jessi's the oldest of three, Mallory of eight (can you imagine?).

Both girls absolutely adore reading, especially horse books. They're not clones, though. Jessi's African-American and an incredibly dedicated ballerina. Her hair is usually pulled back tightly, and she carries herself with elegance and grace. Mal is Caucasian and not very athletic. She has a mop of reddish-brown hair, and she wears glasses and braces. Her great passion is writing and illustrating stories, and she dreams of becoming a children's book author someday.

That's it for our regular members. We do have two associate members, who fill in for us whenever we're super busy. They're not required to attend meetings or pay dues. One of them is Logan, Mary Anne's boyfriend. He's a terrific sitter, but he participates in several after-school sports, so his schedule is always tight. The other is Shannon Kilbourne, who goes to a private school called Stoneybrook Day School and is involved in tons of extracurricular activities.

Back to our meeting. Claudia had disappeared into her closet and was now emerging with a box of Wheat Thins. "So? Did Ms. Hartley need help grading papers or something?"

"She just wanted to bug me about joining Mathletes again," I said. "That's all."

"Cool," Abby remarked.

Somehow, that wasn't among the words I'd expected to hear. *"Cool?"* I repeated.

Abby shrugged. "My school on Long Island had a math team. They were the Nassau County champs. Those kids were so smart."

"You'd be great on that team, Stacey," Mary Anne said.

I shrugged. "Well . . . yeah, I guess. But it's, you know, the *Maaaaathletes.*" I made a scrunched-up nerd face.

Claudia looked puzzled. "Did you just smell something funky?"

"Look, I'm not seriously thinking about it," I replied. "Between homework and baby-sitting and tutoring Lindsey, it would be too much. Besides, it's too geeky."

"It wouldn't be if you joined," Jessi remarked.

"One of us could tutor Lindsey," Mary Anne volunteered.

"What's the commitment?" Kristy asked sharply.

"A month or so," I replied. "Practices are informal, not mandatory. Meets are mostly on weekends."

Kristy relaxed. "In that case, I say go for it."

Mary Anne and Abby nodded in agreement.

"I wish I could do something like that," Claudia said. "Do they have a remedial team?"

"We'll come cheer for you," Jessi offered.

"SMS, SMS! If you don't know the answer, take a guess!" Mallory improvised.

All of a sudden, the idea didn't seem so dumb. I guess I'd really been afraid of Kristy's reaction. Of everyone's reaction. Afraid they'd think I'd gone nerdy on them.

But the more I thought about it, the more ridiculous that seemed. I mean, I've always liked math. I'm talented at it. If I were good in sports, I would join a team. People would come to see me. They'd appreciate my skill. It would feel great. Why should I be deprived of that? If I couldn't be an athlete, why not a Mathlete?

One thought was still sticking in my mind, though. I could probably work Mathletes around baby-sitting and homework but not my tutoring sessions with Lindsey. They were usually right after school, and they were always exhausting. (Lindsey is incredibly stubborn.)

I turned to Mary Anne. "If I did join Mathletes, you wouldn't mind tutoring Lindsey?"

"Well, I said one of us could," Mary Anne replied. "I have to spend so much time with Victoria."

Victoria Kent, by the way, is an eight-year-old princess from England. Her family is living in Stoneybrook for a few months while her parents work at the U.N., and they hired Mary Anne to be Victoria's official "companion."

"I'd do it, if it weren't for all my ballet classes," Jessi said.

"The Krushers are having some indoor preseason practices at Stoneybrook Elementary," Kristy added.

"I have a bunch of orthodontist sessions coming up," Mallory spoke up.

"Transportation problem," said Abby.

We all looked at Claudia.

Her face fell. "Ohhhh, no, you don't."

"You're doing fine in math," Kristy reminded her.

"But — but I — " Claudia sputtered.

"You'll be great at it," Mallory said. "And Lindsey loves you."

"But — "

"Tutoring is a great way to build your confidence too," Mary Anne added. "Remember how much fun you had tutoring Shea Rodowsky?"

"But — "

"It's settled," Kristy announced. "Any further business?"

Claudia sank back against the wall.

She looked like a mouse in a trap.

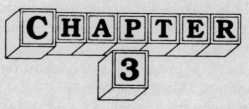

CHAPTER 3

"Stacey, needless to say, I'm *very* pleased!"

That was Ms. Hartley's reaction to my decision. Yup, I joined. I'd spent all of Thursday mulling it over, and just became more and more interested. So I went to Ms. Hartley's room after school, before I could change my mind.

"What's our schedule?" I asked.

"The next practice is tomorrow evening at seven-thirty, at my house," Ms. Hartley said. "I'll provide enough dessert food for everyone."

"Well, actually, I'm diabetic, so I don't eat sweets."

"Then I'll have something you can enjoy too. We'll probably be working pretty hard for Saturday's competition."

"Which I don't have to be in, right?" I said.

"You'll be our ninth member. We only need five for each problem, but we rotate. You can sit out, but I think you'll be ready. We'll go over plenty of questions from previous contests." She stood and shook my hand. "Welcome to the Mathletes."

"Thanks," I said.

I got flutters in my stomach just thinking about the meet. I hate being the center of attention at big events. But this was Mathletes. How big a deal could it be?

Next stop, the mall, to buy a polyester plaid shirt and high-water pants.

Just kidding.

HONNNNNK!

As I stepped out the front door, a car horn blared. I looked toward the curb to see a blue Lincoln Town Car with dark-tinted windows.

HONNNNNK!

Probably some obnoxious high school senior picking up a younger sibling, I figured.

I looked around for my BSC friends. Usually we meet for some after-school gabbing, but I guess they'd all left when I was with Ms. Hartley. So I began walking home alone.

HONNNNNK! HONNNNNK!

Suddenly I realized I was the only student on the sidewalk. And the car was rolling toward me.

I picked up the pace.

"Hey, is this any way to treat the most important man in your life?" a deep voice called out.

The car pulled up beside me. Through the windshield, I could see a familiar smiling face.

"Dad?" I said. "Hi! What — who — ?"

"Like it?" he shouted through the passenger window, which was sliding open.

"Are you here on business or something?" I asked.

"Come on, I'll take you for a spin."

I was smiling so hard my face hurt. My dad in Stoneybrook on a workday? It was a miracle. If you knew him, you'd be shocked too. He's about the hardest-working human being ever born. I can hardly ever reach him by phone during the day.

I opened the door, slid into the front seat, and gave him a kiss. I was so excited, I started babbling. "I hope you're not taking me to a board meeting or something. Does Mom know you're here? Oh, Dad, this is sooooo cool! Are you staying over? Nice rental car they gave you!"

Dad laughed. "Whoa, one thing at a time. Yes, I am staying over, at the Strathmore Inn. No, your mother doesn't know I'm here. No, I have no meetings. And it's not a rental car. I bought it."

"You? A car?"

I should explain. Like most people who live in New York City, my dad doesn't own a car.

He uses subways, buses, and taxis. When he needs to leave town, he uses trains, planes, and rented cars. Period. I'd have been less surprised if he told me he'd bought a hippopotamus.

"Hey, why not?" Dad said with a proud smile. "Why should I be a slave to mass transportation? Why not take to the open road? See the country on my own terms. Be free to spend quality time with my daughter on a moment's notice. Stay the weekend if I want — like this weekend!"

"Seriously?"

"Seriously."

"Yyyyyes!" I said, punching the air.

"How about a movie tomorrow night?"

"Well, after my practice, I guess. Dad, you won't believe this, but I joined the Mathletes. And we're having our first meet on Saturday. Can you come?"

"Mathletes? Like, long-distance calculator toss? Laptop bench press?"

"*Daaa-aaad*, it's a math contest. Kids from different schools solve problems."

"Wouldn't miss it. Hang on!"

Dad tore away from the curb. The car sped down the street, whisper-quiet.

"Perhaps you've noticed the rich Corinthian leather upholstery," Dad said in a voice like a

TV announcer, "along with the superior suspension and the pickup of a computer-controlled V-8 engine . . ."

I was hearing Dad's words, but my mind was suddenly on another track.

Thursday. It was Thursday and my dad was not at work. He was staying the weekend, which meant he was not going back to work on Friday. These things made no sense.

"Dad," I interrupted. "Why are you here?"

"Well, I turned the ignition, stepped on the gas — "

"No, I mean, why aren't you in your office? You didn't lose your job, did you?"

I wasn't totally serious about that. But Dad fell silent and didn't say anything for awhile. I could feel my heart sinking.

As Dad pulled up to a red light, he finally spoke. "The company's been having some rough times. They can only let go of just so many middle managers before they hit the vice presidents."

"You were *fired*?"

"Downsized." Dad gave a half-grin. "It's what they call it to make themselves feel better."

"But — but that's awful!" I exclaimed.

The light turned green and Dad turned toward the center of Stoneybrook. "Nah, it's a blessing in disguise. I've been working too hard, anyway. Besides, how difficult do you think it'll be for a guy like me to find another job? I'll walk down Madison Avenue, and the CEOs will be screaming out their windows, 'McGill! McGill! Up here!' Meanwhile, I'll live it up, concentrate on the important things in life, like being a dad. So tell me, do you really like the car? Because if you don't, I'm taking it back."

Wow. For a man who'd been fired, or sized down, Dad seemed in a great mood. "It's nice, if you like blue."

"You hate it! Tomorrow I'm trading it in for a pink Ferraro."

"Ferrari."

"Whatever. Let's celebrate. The Rosebud Cafe?"

"Sure."

Zoom. Off we went.

I barely remember what we talked about at the Rosebud. I know we had a fun time and laughed a lot. But I also know the situation felt weird.

All my life, whenever I thought of Dad, I thought of work. When he and Mom were together, we'd sometimes wait and wait for him at restaurants, and Mom would call to find out he couldn't join us because of a company emergency. Often I'd be asleep at night by the time he came home. I can't tell you how many weekend plans were canceled because of Dad's job. Is it strange to live with a father and always *miss* him? That's how I felt. As you can imagine, the feeling didn't improve after the divorce.

And now, here I was, alone with him on a Thursday. With his undivided attention until at least Saturday.

Who was I to complain? I was thrilled.

Maybe he was right. Unemployment was good for him. He was like a new person. The New Dad.

Dad bellowed with laughter when I called him that at the restaurant. After we wolfed down some cheese, crackers, and juice, blabbering a mile a minute, he said, "I don't know about you, but I'm still starving."

"Go ahead and order a meal," I suggested.

Dad thought about it a minute. "How about I make dinner — at the McGill house?"

That was the last thing I expected to hear. My mom and dad did not have what you'd call a friendly divorce. "Uh . . . right, Dad," I said.

"I'm serious. Your mom and I have been much nicer to each other over the phone lately. Last time I spoke with her, we even had a laugh or two."

"Does she know you're here?"

"No. It'll be a surprise. Look, Stacey, I'm offering to make a gourmet meal. She'll appreciate that after a long day's work. And if she doesn't, I'll leave quietly. You two can enjoy the meal, no hard feelings." Dad smiled broadly. "The New Dad. I really like that name."

I tried to smile back, but boy, did I have my doubts.

Since the divorce, Mom has never liked to talk to Dad. I can always tell when she picks up his phone calls. Her face goes cloudy, she immediately calls out, "Stacey, your dad!" and leaves the phone on the counter for me to pick up.

I had to admit, though, that lately she had actually been talking to him a little. She hadn't exactly been bubbly, but she hadn't seemed as if she wanted to kill him anymore. That was a good sign.

Maybe Dad was right. Maybe Mom would appreciate this kind of surprise. I sure would have liked to see them reach a truce.

It was worth a try.

We finished up and left. First stop was the fish store, where Dad bought some humongous lobsters. Then we went to a fruit and vegetable market for some exotic greens and imported fruit. Next stop was home.

I loved having Dad in the house, but I couldn't help feeling a little tense. So I put on a CD of my favorite group, U4Me. Dad and I assembled a green salad together, dancing to the tunes (Dad tried to sing along, but he was too dorky for words). Then we melted some butter and boiled the lobsters (gross, gross, gross — but good, good, good).

We'd set the table and lit two candles when the doorbell rang.

"I'll get it!" we both shouted.

We raced for the door. I was cracking up. New Dad was acting like a big kid.

Together we yanked the door open.

"Sorry, my hands were full and I didn't want to dig the keys out of my pocket," Mom said in a rush. "Who is that parked in our driveway?"

When she saw Dad, she stopped short.

"Surprise," he said.

"What are *you* doing here?" Mom asked.

"Fixing dinner." Dad took Mom's bags and headed into the kitchen. Putting on a terrible French accent, he called over his shoulder, "Yourrr waitair weel be weeth you in a moment, madame."

Mom looked dumbfounded. "Stacey, what's going on?"

"Well, you see, Dad was — " I began.

"Notheeng like a leetle downsizeeng to poot ze unemployed chef back in zee keetchen!" Dad called out.

32

"Whaaaat?" Mom threw her down coat on the living room sofa and ran into the kitchen. "You're not serious?"

"Ah am, mah formair sweetheart!"

"Stop that, Ed. Talk to me. How could they fire you? What are you going to do?"

As I walked into the kitchen, Dad was handing her a plate with a steaming red lobster on it. "I intend to rejoice," he announced. "Become a renowned chef. A kinder ex-husband. A fantastic New Dad."

"You don't mind if Dad stays for dinner, do you?" I asked.

"I — I don't suppose I have much choice," Mom replied. "Where are you staying, Ed?"

"He's staying at the Strathmore this weekend and coming to my Mathletes meet," I said.

Mom gave him a wary smile. "Mmm-hmm. Great."

"Shall we?" Dad said, holding up his plate. "These lobos won't stay hot forever."

Together we walked into the living room. Dad was humming along with U4Me. Mom? Well, let's just say she was trying hard to look pleasant.

Usually she likes surprises. But I could tell she wasn't crazy about this one.

Oh, well. She hadn't stomped away in anger. She hadn't thrown him out.

Hope, hope, hope.

It was so great to see Dad. I wanted to make the most of it. I knew that as soon as he found a new job, he'd be a stranger again.

Might as well live it up while you can.

I sat down and dug in. Lobster never tasted so good.

CHAPTER 4

"Excuse me."

In the car on the way to Ms. Hartley's house, I couldn't stop burping. Mom and I had feasted on leftovers from the previous night's dinner with Dad. I'd brushed my teeth, gargled, and downed three sugarless mints, but my breath still smelled like lobster.

I don't think Mom noticed. She was staring intently at the road, gripping the steering wheel tightly. "So, what time do you think you'll be home?"

"Well, the practice is supposed to take an hour and a half," I replied, "and then Dad's picking me up to make a nine-twenty movie, so . . . I guess eleven-thirty, eleven-forty?"

"And you have a meet and a sitting job tomorrow?" Mom let out a big sigh. "Honestly, I will never understand your father."

"I don't have to get up *that* early, Mom. I'll get enough sleep. Dad just wants to spend time with me before he finds another job. I mean, I am his daughter."

"I know, sweetheart. It's just that — well, you know the way he is. Buying that new car, the hotel, the lobsters, peaches and plums in February — "

"What do peaches and plums have to do with it?"

"They're out of season. Which means they must have been imported. That makes them very expensive. Like everything he's buying. It's not a healthy pattern, Stacey. An unemployed person can't throw money around. What if he doesn't find a job for awhile?"

"Well, what's he supposed to do, sit around and mope while he's waiting?"

Mom chuckled. "Not your father. He'll just attack joblessness the way he attacks his work. Frantic. Go, go, go. Let nothing or no one stand in his way."

I could not believe my mother was being so harsh. It brought back a rush of bad memories, of arguments she and Dad used to have before they were divorced.

As we pulled in front of Ms. Hartley's house, I pushed the car door open. "Well, I'm glad he's here."

"I know you are," Mom said softly. "I don't mean to be so negative. I do care about your dad, believe it or not. I just hope he knows how to pace himself during the rough times coming up."

"I guess some people need to have a little faith," I replied, closing the door firmly.

Walking up the steps to Ms. Hartley's house, I felt guilty. I turned to wave at Mom as she drove away, but she didn't see me.

Oh, well. She was just sore at Dad for stealing me away. Believe me, I've been through that before. It's one of the worst things about being a Divorced Kid. I could predict that Mom and I were going to have a loooong talk at midnight about it.

I tried to put Dad and Mom out of my mind. I was feeling nervous about the Mathletes.

Who was on the team? I had no idea. It seemed like some kind of secret society. Maybe no one wanted to admit being a member. Maybe they were all pimply little gnomes with unwashed hair and Coke-bottle glasses. Maybe neighbors were taking secret photos of me, to be seen in the *Stoneybrook News* under the headline POPULAR SMS BABY-SITTER TRANSFORMS INTO SUPERNERD.

Maybe it wasn't too late to chase Mom down.

Stop it, I said to myself.

I held my head high and rang the doorbell.

Ms. Hartley yanked the door open. She was wearing jeans, an SMS sweatshirt, and a great big smile. "Welcome! Come on downstairs. Everyone's eager to see you."

I followed her through the house. When we reached the kitchen, she took a foil-covered plate off the counter and handed it to me. "These are sugar-free cookies and pastries from my favorite shop, In Good Taste. The owner's husband is diabetic, and he devised the recipes himself."

Boy, was I impressed. I knew all about these pastries (and I love them). "Thanks," I said.

"I'm sure you'll recognize a lot of faces," Ms. Hartley went on, leading me into the basement. "Jason Fox, Alexander Kurtzman . . ."

Yikes! Dork Alert! Jason, the sports statistics freak who pesters the basketball team. Alexander, the only eighth-grader who carries a briefcase to school and wears a jacket and tie.

We were not off to a good start.

". . . Emily Bernstein, Gordon Brown, Rick Chow," Ms. Hartley continued, "Mari Drabek, Bea Foster, and Amanda Martin."

By now we were in the basement. There was no turning back. (Which was okay, since I felt a little better about the rest of the kids.) Jason was pumping his fist in the air and dancing around, shouting, "Yyyyyes! Three cheers! Secant, tangent, cosine, sine . . . three point one four one five nine . . . Stacey! Stacey! Stacey!"

Alexander pushed his glasses up his nose

and grinned so hard his braces nearly blinded me. "Three point one four one five nine . . . you know? The value of *pi*?"

Puh-leeze.

"Hi," I managed to murmur.

Mari gently took the platter from me. She set it down on a Ping-Pong table, next to some other food platters. Rick was writing PROPERTY OF STACEY ONLY in thick marker on a sheet of paper.

I smiled at Mari. I sure was glad she was in the group. I knew her pretty well. During a school trip to Hawaii, we were involved in a helicopter accident together.

I also knew Emily Bernstein, who runs the school newspaper. And Bea Foster, who is about the smartest math student I ever met. Rick and I were on a committee for a school masquerade party. All of them are pretty cool.

Four out of eight wasn't bad. I didn't know Amanda and Gordon that well. And Jason and Alexander weren't terrible people, really. Just strange.

I had hope. I vowed to keep my heart and mind open. I would not *not NOT* be a snob.

"Hey, what did the maple seed say when it started to grow?" Jason blurted out. "Give up? *Geometry!* Get it? Gee, I'm a tree!"

(It was not *not NOT* going to be easy.)

"*Fo-o-o-ox!*" groaned Rick.

"Ignore him, Stacey," Emily said.

"Okay, everybody pull up chairs." Ms. Hartley pushed the food into the middle of the Ping-Pong table and slapped down a manila folder. "Here are copies of last year's local championship questions. As you know, Stoneybrook Day School won, and we're facing them tomorrow — as well as Kelsey Middle School. They're both tough teams, and — "

"Tough?" Jason snorted. "Uh, riiiight."

"Be serious," Alexander whispered.

As we dragged chairs to the table and sat, Ms. Hartley said, "Stacey, the meet will be held in the auditorium at Stoneybrook Day School. Basically, there are two types of problems: individual and Mathmania. The individual problems are timed, and everyone works privately. If you get the answer, you receive one point and so does your team. The team with the most points wins the problem. The Mathmania problems are untimed. The team solves them together, the first team to find the answer receives five points, and each member receives one point toward his or her individual total. At the end of the tournament a prize will be awarded for the highest team score and the highest individual score. Got that?"

I nodded. Seemed simple enough.

"Okay, let's start." Ms. Hartley pulled out a sheet with this shape drawn on it:

"This cube is made out of blocks," Ms. Hartley said. "The entire cube is painted blue. How many blocks have blue paint on them?"

"Does it matter how many sides of the block are painted?" Emily asked.

"No," Ms. Hartley replied. "A block with any amount of paint counts."

Jason was scribbling in a notebook. "Twenty-seven!" he shouted. "Three blocks long times three blocks wide times three blocks deep. That makes twenty-seven. *EHHHHH!* And Jason Fox wins a trip to Disney World! Yeeeeaaaaa! The crowd goes wild!"

"Anyone else?" Ms. Hartley asked.

"I'm with Jason," Gordon agreed.

I looked at the cube carefully. The answer seemed so obvious.

"Twenty-six," I said.

Jason howled. "Uh, hello? Where were you when they taught the times tables?"

"One of the blocks is buried in the middle," I explained. "It has no paint on it."

Total silence.

Ms. Hartley was beaming. "Good thinking, Stacey."

Jason looked as though he'd just swallowed a baby porcupine. "I knew that. I just wanted to see if you did."

Rick bopped him over the head with a rolled-up spiral notebook.

"All riiiight, Stace," Mari whispered.

"Just lucky," I said modestly.

"Okay, now, who can fill in the next number of this sequence?" Ms. Hartley spread out a sheet of paper that contained these numbers:

$$1 \quad 2 \quad 4 \quad 7 \quad 12 \quad 19 \quad 30 \quad 43 \quad \underline{\quad}$$

Scribble, scribble, scribble.

"Are you sure this isn't a mistake?" Amanda asked.

"I get fifty-eight," Bea volunteered.

I had a different answer. I looked at Bea's page and saw all kinds of fancy calculations. I felt sort of stupid. Maybe I was missing a trick.

Jason looked over my shoulder and read my paper. "Sixty?" he read. "How did you get that?"

"Well," I replied, "take the differences between the numbers. You get one, two, three, five, seven, eleven, and thirteen. Those are all prime numbers. The next prime number is seventeen. So you add that to forty-three and get sixty."

"Exactly!" Ms. Hartley exclaimed.

Emily burst into applause. "Whoa, this girl is hot!"

"Stoneybrook Day and Kelsey Middle, you *die* tomorrow!" Rick cried out.

Jason fell to his knees and began salaaming at my feet.

Weird.

Très weird.

But I have to admit, I was enjoying it.

Ms. Hartley kept feeding us problems, one after the other. The session sped by. (No, I did not get every one right. I made an addition error on the second to last one. Hey, I'm human.)

When Ms. Hartley called the end of the session, I groaned. "I was just warming up."

"You mean, you can be even smarter?" Emily asked.

"It boggles the mind," Alexander muttered.

"I say we let her and Bea answer all the questions," Amanda suggested.

Jason nodded. "Yeah, the rest of us can just smile and look beautiful."

"Let's hear it for the Stace!" Gordon called out.

"YEEEEAAAA!" cried the other Mathletes.

I was blushing. I could feel it. It was nice to be appreciated for my brain.

Nice? I was almost floating.

"All right, the meet is at one o'clock tomorrow at Stoneybrook Day," Ms. Hartley said.

"I'd like to have a brushup session in my classroom at eleven-thirty."

Thump. I was down on the ground again.

I had agreed to help Mallory baby-sit for the Pike kids and their friends before the meet.

As my teammates put their coats on, I said to Ms. Hartley, "What if I can't make the brushup? I mean, I have a good excuse. I have to do this baby-sitting job and — "

Ms. Hartley put a calming hand on my arm. "Not to worry. This isn't the Olympics. We're in this for the fun."

"But I might not be prepared enough for the meet — "

"Stacey," Ms. Hartley interrupted. "You're prepared. The other teams aren't going to know what hit them."

Whew.

I felt about ten feet tall as I left the house.

Dad was waiting for me, as promised, with a big smile on his face and a gardenia for my hair.

Was I lucky, or what?

Friday

Okay, I kno your all wating with bated breth. You stayed up all nite wondering what hapened. Your dying to kno the story of Claudia the Tooter.

I dont blaim you. Before today, I never tooted anybody in math. How did I feel, walking into Linsy's house? Horified! I thot I was going to feint. In fact, I would have run away, if it hadnt' been for the ~~Aloxam Atgoba~~ Altoxam Big Foot...

"**Y**aaahh-hah-hah!" screamed Buddy Barrett, jumping out of the bushes near his front porch. "I'm the Abdominable Snowman!"

Claudia nearly jumped out of her coat. She was already scared out of her mind. She'd been standing at the Barrett/DeWitts' front door for about three minutes. Frozen. Trying to find the nerve to ring the bell.

As you can see by her BSC notebook entry, Claudia was having doubts about tutoring Lindsey. If Buddy hadn't appeared, she might have run right to Ms. Hartley's house and yanked me out of the basement.

"Buddy, you nearly gave me a heart attack!" Claudia said. "And it's *Abominable*. I think."

The front door opened and Mrs. DeWitt peered out. "Hi, Claudia. Did Big Foot attack you?"

"Rrrraaaagh!" Buddy yelled. He was wearing a down coat with a furry collar and a black ski mask over his face.

Buddy, by the way, is eight. So's Lindsey DeWitt. They're the oldest of seven kids in a blended family. That's *blended* as in *from two marriages*, not as in *mixed smoothly*. Buddy has two sisters, a five-year-old named Suzi and a two-year-old named Marnie. Lindsey's siblings are Taylor (six), Madeleine (four), and Ryan (two). Luckily for Claudia, Taylor, Madeleine, Byan, and Marnie were all at friends' houses, so Claudia only had three kids to sit for.

Lindsey came running into the living room, calling out, "Did you scare her away?"

"Nahhh," Buddy replied.

Lindsey took one look at Claudia and slumped. "You *dork!*"

"Lindsey, is that any way to talk to your tutor?" asked Mrs. DeWitt.

"I was talking to Cruddy Buddy!" Lindsey replied, stomping away.

"Heyyy!" Buddy cried, running in after her.

Mrs. DeWitt gave Claudia a sympathetic look. "Good luck."

Her husband bounced into the room, carrying two winter coats. "Hi. Where's Stacey?"

"Claudia's taking her place," Mrs. DeWitt answered. "Stacey joined the Mathletes team, so she's busy."

Mr. DeWitt is a nice, easygoing guy. He insists that we call him by his first name, Franklin. But when he heard the news, he looked about as friendly as a cactus. "Oh. So . . . this is not a tutoring session? It's just baby-sitting?"

"No, I'm tuting," Claudia said. "I mean, tutoring."

"Oh. Okay," said Franklin's mouth. His face, however, was saying, *You? A kid who flunked out of eighth grade? Some bargain.* (At least that's how Claudia took it.)

Not exactly terrific for the old self-confidence.

Franklin and Mrs. DeWitt gave Claudia some last-minute instructions and zipped off to a PTO meeting.

Claudia walked inside, clutching a manila folder full of my notes to Lindsey.

The house, as usual, was in chaos. In the kitchen, Suzi was scooping ice cream into bowls, while Buddy was in the family room, rummaging through video cassettes.

"Mom said we're all supposed to watch *Babe* while you teach Lindsey," Buddy announced.

"No fair!" cried Lindsey's voice from behind a closed door upstairs.

Claudia helped Suzi clean up assorted ice-cream toppings then plopped Suzi and Buddy in front of the TV. As *Babe* oinked onto the screen, she walked upstairs and knocked on Lindsey's door.

"I'm too tired to study!" was Lindsey's greeting.

Claudia gently pushed the door open. Lindsey was curled up on her bed, in her clothes, her eyes tightly shut.

"Don't worry, I left my torture equipment at home," Claudia said.

Lindsey opened her eyes. "No, you didn't. It's right in your hand."

Claudia set the folder down on the floor and

knelt by Lindsey's bed. "You know, math was my absolute worst subject. When I was in third grade, I'd rather have eaten roasted shoe leather than done my homework."

"So why are you tutoring me?" Lindsey snapped.

"I'm much better at it now," Claudia replied. "Besides, I have Stacey's notes."

"I don't care," Lindsey declared. "They all get to watch a video, and *I* have to do stupid math! Besides, kids aren't required to do homework on a Friday. Everybody knows that."

"Let's make a deal," Claudia said. "Learn what Stacey planned for today, then you can run downstairs and watch."

"But it's too hard!"

"No, it's not." Claudia opened the notes and began reading: " 'In problems involving estimation, rounding up is done with numbers half or greater than the value of the place of estimation. That is, five or more if the place is tens, fifty or more if it's hundreds, and so on. For example, eight hundred thirty seven, rounded to the tens place, would round *up*, to eight hundred forty; but to the hundreds, it would round *down* to eight hundred.' "

"I don't understand *that!*" Lindsey exclaimed.

Claudia took a deep breath. "Neither do I."

"See?"

"Let me teach it my way." Claudia wrote 837 on a sheet of paper. "What's this closest to?" Under the number she wrote 820, 830, 840, and 850.

"I hate math!"

"The answer is eight hundred twenty."

Lindsey glared at her. "Is not. It's eight forty."

"Why?"

"Because thirty-seven is close to forty."

"Okay, that's if you round to the tens. What about these numbers?" Claudia scribbled 700, 800, 900. "Which is it closer to now?"

Lindsey exhaled. "Eight hundred. That's easy."

"You just did exactly what Stacey was saying."

"I did?"

"Yup." Claudia scanned my notes again. " 'Addition and subtraction, using estimation.' Hmmm . . . Let's do this Claudia-style."

(Okay, time-out. I ask you, was my description that awful? *Precise* is the way I would put it. But when I told that to Claudia, she just laughed. She said I was much better at understanding than explaining. Hmmph.)

Anyway, "Claudia-style" seemed to work fine for Lindsey. In a few minutes, she was adding and subtracting three-digit numbers, using estimation.

Next unit, subtracting three-digit numbers

for real. Claudia copied down problems I had written and gave Lindsey a quiz. This is how she answered:

$$457 - 368 = 111$$ $$900 - 406 = 506$$ $$720 - 619 = 119$$

"Now can I go downstairs?" Lindsey asked.

"Uh, Lindsey, hasn't anyone told you about borrowing?" Claudia said.

Lindsey scowled. "I didn't want to!"

"Well, you have to!" Claudia dove into a big box of Legos near Lindsey's bed. "Okay, each yellow Lego equals one. Red Legos equal ten, blue a hundred. Let's set up problem one."

She lined up enough blocks to form the number 457. "Okay, start with the ones column. We have seven yellows and we have to take away eight. What do we do?"

"Start in the hundreds column. That one's easier."

"Neeeahhh, Doc," Claudia replied in a Bugs Bunny voice. "Right to left. Dat's the rule."

Using the Legos (and silly voices), Claudia demonstrated the concept of borrowing. (The tens were a family of Elmer Fudds, the hundreds were Yosemite Sams.)

Claudia went through every cartoon character she could think of. Then she started singing the rules, to the tune of "On Top of Old Smokey":

"If you can't subtraaaact it,
Then borrow a one,
And in the next co-o-olumn,
Reduce it by one!"

No, it won't make the Top Forty. But Lindsey loved it. In fact, she made Claudia go to the third-grade textbook for more problems.

That video? Forgotten. Lindsey was so excited to be finding answers, she wouldn't stop.

When the front door opened, Lindsey bolted downstairs.

Claudia followed her, past the family room, which still echoed with bleating and barking from the movie.

Franklin and Mrs. DeWitt were standing with the rest of the Barrett/DeWitt brood inside the front door. "Mom! Dad!" Lindsey shouted. "I can borrow!"

"Uh, excuse me, honey?" Franklin said.

"Come on, Claudia," Lindsey urged, bursting into song. "Don't borrow a zeeero . . . just turn it to niiiine . . . skip to the next co-o-olumn . . . the number you'll find . . ."

Mrs. DeWitt looked totally baffled. "Uh, very nice."

"We can prove it with Legos!" Lindsey continued. "I'll show you!"

As she ran upstairs, Claudia squirmed. "It was the only thing I could think of. I mean, I know we were supposed to use Stacey's notes . . ."

Franklin carefully took off his coat. He and Mrs. DeWitt exchanged a Look.

"I can ask Stacey to come back," Claudia blabbered on. "Maybe now that she knows her schedule — "

"Not necessary," Franklin cut her off. "Claudia, I've never seen Lindsey like this about math."

Mrs. DeWitt was beaming. "You're a miracle worker. When can you come back? Strictly as a tutor, I mean. We'd be here to take care of the rest of the kids."

Claudia nearly died. She signed up two more sessions on the spot.

How did I feel about that? Did I mind being forgotten like an old toy? All my hard work tossed aside?

Not *moi*. When Claudia told me, I was gracious, calm, and grateful.

I only snarled after she hung up.

Oh, well, I guess sometimes you gotta have a gimmick.

CHAPTER 6

"Do you have a packet of honey?" Mom asked, pushing open the front door of Stoneybrook Day School.

"Yes, Mom," I replied.

"Did you eat enough lunch?"

"Yes, Mom."

"Did you finish studying that review sheet Ms. Hartley gave you?"

"Yes, Mom."

"I don't know why I'm so nervous. You should be the one who's nervous. Are you nervous?"

I did not answer the question. I couldn't. My teeth were clenched in fear. Besides, at that moment, Mom was swallowed up by the huge throng in the school lobby.

Well, maybe not a throng. But many more people than I had expected.

Okay, Ms. Hartley had warned me. She'd said it was an important event. But somehow

I imagined a few parents and siblings sitting around, checking their watches every few minutes. Not Oscar night in Stoneybrook.

How did I feel?

Petrified.

I looked around for familiar faces. None. Zippo. Frankly, I don't know any Kelsey Middle School kids. And my only SDS friends are Shannon Kilbourne, our BSC associate, and Bart Taylor, Kristy's friend. Oh, and a few elementary-age kids (unlike SMS, Stoneybrook Day goes from kindergarten through twelfth grade).

A lobby full of strangers. All there to see me perform. Like a seal in the zoo.

The front door beckoned. Escape. A list of excuses ran though my mind. I forgot my calculator. I had a diabetic reaction. Part of the school ceiling fell and conked me on the head.

"Heyyyy, there's the champ!"

Honestly, if I hadn't heard my dad's voice, I might have bolted. He was elbowing through the crowd, holding a bouquet of flowers.

I unclenched my jaw. "Hi, Dad."

"Darn," he said, frowning at the bouquet. "You're so beautiful, you make these look ugly."

I couldn't help laughing. "You are so corny."

Dad took my arm and we walked through the auditorium entrance together. Mom and

Ms. Hartley were chatting behind the last row of seats.

As we approached them, the famous Kristy Thomas two-fingered whistle sounded.

PHWEEEEEEET!

The room fell silent for a moment.

"Yo! Over here! I saved seats!" yelled Kristy, waving to us from the front row. Mary Anne, Logan, Jessi, Mallory, Claudia, and Abby were sitting with her. Behind them, coats were draped over a few seats.

Everyone was staring at us. I was mortified.

Mom, Dad, Ms. Hartley, and I exchanged a flurry of good-byes and good lucks. As my parents sat in the audience, I walked onto the stage.

Way in the back of the stage, custodians were setting up a huge *Wheel of Fortune*–type contraption. It was divided into math categories: geometry and measurement, number patterns, logic, factors and divisibility, fractions, and odds 'n' ends. On the far left of the stage was a table with an overhead projector and screen. The three team tables formed a rough U shape in the center of the stage. Each contestant's place was marked with a tented placard, a pad of paper, and several pencils. In the middle of each table was a large, old-fashioned handbell.

SMS was in the middle. As I approached the

table, Emily, Gordon, and Rick were hunched together, poring over sample questions.

Emily was the first to see me. "I am *so* glad you're here," was her greeting. "What's a Fibonacci sequence?"

Gulp.

We'd gone over that in the practice session. But did I remember it? No. "It — isn't it — uh, wait — "

While I fumbled, Bea walked onto the stage. Emily repeated the question, and Bea quickly wrote down the numbers 1, 1, 2, 3, 5, 8, and 13. "Add the first two numbers to get the third," she whispered. "The second two numbers to get the fourth, and so on."

"Yeah," I said. "That's it."

Brilliant, Stacey.

I calmly sat in my seat, trying to keep my knees from knocking.

"*Sta-cey*! Sta-*cey*! Sta-*cey*!" Kristy shouted at the top of her lungs.

Abby was punching the air in rhythm. Claudia was doing a little dance. Jessi was staring at them as if they'd lost their minds. Mallory and Mary Anne were blushing. Logan looked as if he wanted to barf.

Behind them sat Mom and Dad, deep in conversation. I wondered what they were talking about. Me? Dad's job prospects? My loud friends?

In this atmosphere, I was supposed to think?

I tried to keep calm. I chatted with my team-mates. I greeted the others as they walked onto the stage. I must have been forming coherent words, because no one took my temperature and rushed me offstage. But I cannot remember one word of any conversation.

I was a wreck.

When everyone was seated, the lights dimmed and a stocky man with a bow tie strolled onto the stage. "I'm Reverty Schmidt, head of the math department at Stoneybrook Day," he announced.

A small cheer went up from the crowd.

"Reverty Schmidt?" Rick whispered.

I could see shoulders bobbing to my right and left. I tried not to crack up.

As Mr. Schmidt read from a pad of paper, his hands were shaking. "And so, in conclusion . . ." He squinted and shuffled the papers around. "Sorry. Er, welcome to Stoneybrook Day School."

The audience burst into laughter. Mr. Schmidt smiled and shrugged. "I'm much better with numbers," he muttered.

Somehow, watching Mr. Schmidt stumble through his speech calmed me down. He was more nervous than I was.

"Uh, the contest today involves sixteen problems altogether," Mr. Schmidt droned on.

"In groups of four. Now, how many groups is that, folks?"

"Five!" Claudia shouted. "I mean, four!"

"Uh, give that person a rubber chicken," Mr. Schmidt read from his sheet. He looked up as if he expected laughter. (No such luck.) "Ahem. The teams take turns spinning the math wheel. I will read a problem in whatever category the wheel stops on. The players work in silence for three minutes, then show their answers. Each correct answer is one point for the player's team, and one point for the individual player. Every fourth problem is 'Mathmania' and has no time limit. Team members can consult with one another. Five points go to the first team that rings the bell and gives a correct answer, and each player on that team receives an individual point. And now, without further ado, I will ask a member of the Stoneybrook Middle School team to step to the wheel."

I felt Ms. Hartley nudge me from behind. "Go ahead, Stacey."

"Whup 'em, Stace!" cried Kristy from the audience.

I swallowed hard. I stood up, walked to the wheel, and spun.

It stopped at geometry and measurement.

As I went back to my seat, Mr. Schmidt read: " 'George has three rods that are seven inches, ten inches, and twelve inches long. How can he use them to measure something fifteen inches long?' Okay . . . go!"

Huh?

My snowy, short-circuited mind creaked into action.

If you put the ten-inch and seven-inch rods together, they measured seventeen inches. Too long.

Quickly I drew the rods in different configurations. By the time the bell rang, I'd drawn this:

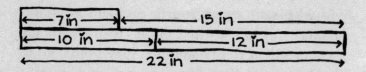

"Okay, sign your answers and place them in front of you," Mr. Schmidt said.

When we did, he posted the correct answer on the overhead projector.

My answer!

"Yea!" I shouted.

"Gimme an *S!*" Kristy shouted. (Someone must have calmed her down, because she didn't reach *T.*)

Mr. Schmidt hurried around the stage, marking down all of our scores. "Stoneybrook Day . . . five. Kelsey . . . four. Stoneybrook Middle . . . three."

Jason and Emily looked upset. I, however, was

feeling much better. I leaned over to them and whispered, "Hang on, we're going to win this!"

Someone from Kelsey spun next. The category was number patterns. Mr. Schmidt put these numbers on the overhead projector:

$$2 \square 4 = 8$$
$$4 \square 1 = 17$$
$$3 \square 3 = 12$$
$$2 \square 5 = 9$$
$$6 \square 7 = \underline{\hspace{1cm}}$$

"Figure out what process goes in the square," Mr. Schmidt read. "Hint: it may be more than one operation. Use that process to solve the last statement."

I could hear Claudia muttering, "No way."

Looking at the first problem, I figured the box could mean *multiply the first number by two, then add the second*. But if that were true, then the answer to the second problem would have to be 9, not 17.

I fiddled around some more, and then it dawned on me. Can you figure it out? (If you said, *square* the first number, then add the second, you were right.)

This time, four SDS students answered correctly, four from Kelsey — and *all five* of us. We were gaining!

The rest of the meet shot by. We lost the first

Mathmania problem, which really set us back. Then SDS picked up steam. By the last problem, SDS had 65 points, we had 61, and Kelsey had 61.

The last problem was Mathmania. Five points. The winner would take the game. We all leaned in toward each other as Jason spun.

The wheel stopped on geometry and measurement again.

"You have ten rosebushes," Mr. Schmidt read. "Plant them in five rows, with only four bushes in each row."

The other teams started yakking and scribbling furiously.

Jason plopped back down in his seat. "Trick question," he said.

"No kidding," Emily replied. "Five rows, four bushes? That makes twenty bushes!"

"You have to double up," Bea offered.

"Duh," was Jason's response.

Rick drew a triangle shape and placed dots on it to represents bushes. Jason drew a kind of double X. Bea worked on a six-sided star.

"That's it!" I said. I experimented with star shapes until I drew this:

"Five sides, each with four dots!" I exclaimed.

Bea picked up the bell and rang.

You should have seen the looks on the other two teams' faces. A guy on the Kelsey team banged his table. A girl from SDS groaned so loudly I thought she was hurt.

Mr. Schmidt ran to me and picked up my sheet. Carefully he looked it over and announced: "Five points for the SMS team. So . . . the final score is, Kelsey Middle School, sixty-one; Stoneybrook Day, sixty-five; and Stoneybrook Middle, sixty-seven!"

"YEEEEEAAAAAAA!" screamed the front row.

Mari threw her arms around me, then Bea. Soon the entire team was in a group hug. Jason broke away and started doing a goony, rubber-legged victory dance. (Any other time it would have made me want to puke. This time, I didn't mind it a bit.)

"Congratulations to the new Stoneybrook eighth-grade math champions!" Mr. Schmidt yelled over the din.

Soon Ms. Hartley was on the stage, embracing us one by one. "I am soooo proud of you," she said into my ear.

You know what? I was proud, too.

"For she's a jolly good Mathlete, for she's a jolly good Mathlete . . ." Kristy was singing.

Abby joined in, and then Mom and Dad. I jumped off the stage and ran to them.

"You were sensational!" Dad exclaimed.

"I was so nervous!" I replied.

"You didn't look it," Claudia said. "I mean, after the first question or so."

"Before then, I was about to call an ambulance," Abby remarked.

We chatted excitedly for awhile. Ms. Hartley joined us, and so did some of my teammates' families.

I was exhausted as I walked outside with Mom and Dad. It was still afternoon, but the sky had that strange dark whiteness that can only mean snow.

"Your chariot awaits, my champion," Dad announced, holding out his arm for me to take.

"If we go straight home," Mom said, "I can start the pot roast right away."

Dad stopped walking. "Oh. Well, actually, I was going to take Stacey into the city. Dinner at Cafe des Artistes. Remember?"

Mom looked at him blankly. "You didn't mention this."

"Didn't I?" Dad asked.

(He hadn't. At least I hadn't remembered it. Typical Dad.)

Mom chuckled patiently. "Look, Ed, things

have been busy. Signals do cross. I propose a compromise: I cook the roast, you stay and eat with us."

Dad took a deep breath. "Well . . . it's just that my reservation is for three."

I knew what that meant. Dinner for Dad, me, and his girlfriend, Samantha.

Mom knew it, too. I could see her face tighten. "I see. Okay, you go ahead. The roast will last another day."

"I knew you'd understand, Maureen," Dad said. "I'll be clearer next time. And I'll bring Stacey back first thing tomorrow."

"Have a wonderful time."

Dad took my arm and led me toward his car. " 'Bye, Maureen."

" 'Bye, Mom!" I shouted.

" 'Bye."

Mom's mouth was smiling. But her eyes weren't.

As I climbed into the car, my great victory feeling was already starting to grow hollow.

CHAPTER 7

*H*onnnnnk! *Honnnnnk!*

"Ed, please, slow down," said Samantha Young.

"Did you see what that cabbie did?" Dad shouted. "He cut off three lanes to make that turn!"

In the backseat, I was clutching the armrest. My knuckles were turning white. As we zipped down Central Park West, the trees of the park were a blur.

I have trotted down the New York City streets in horse-drawn carriages, with drivers speeding all around. I have zoomed across town in cabs that somehow weave and jerk through bumper-to-bumper traffic. I've narrowly avoided accidents at least a dozen times.

But I have never been so scared as I was that Saturday evening in my dad's new car.

"Hey, that was a red light!" Dad shouted angrily out the window to a biker.

I won't even tell you what the biker said in response.

Samantha turned and smiled at me over her shoulder. "I think your father has found his new calling — New York City cab driver."

"I keep forgetting if the restaurant is on West Sixty-seventh Street or Sixty-eighth," Dad growled.

"I don't know," Samantha said.

I looked out the window. The side streets were whipping by us. Cafe des Artistes is my absolute favorite restaurant, and I could see the familiar entrance as we passed it.

"There it is!" I shouted.

Bad move.

EEEEEEE . . . went the brakes of my father's car.

EEEEEEE . . . went the brakes of the car behind us.

HONNNNNNNNK! blasted several horns.

"Ed!" cried Samantha in shock.

My dad was eyeing the curb across the street. "Is that a space?"

"Fire hydrant," I replied.

"Ooh, I see one!" Dad pressed the accelerator and the car lurched forward.

The opening was a block away, and by the time we arrived, another car had made a U-turn from across the street and was nosing into the space.

"You creep!" Dad shouted. *"Didn't you see me?"*

"He can't hear you, Dad," I said softly.

Samantha was shaking her head. "Ed, please, just put it in a garage."

"At those rip-off rates?" Dad replied. "Garages are only for out-of-towners."

Zoom. We were screeching around the block. The side street was crammed with parked cars, so Dad pulled up next to a parking meter on Broadway.

We climbed out, and Dad fed the meter with quarters. "This'll be a fraction of the cost of a garage," he said proudly.

Samantha sighed with relief. "At least we can all relax."

As we strolled down West Sixty-seventh, snow fell lightly, muffling the traffic noise. The trees that lined the sidewalk were decked out with white lights, and a piano sounded from a window across the street. Dad and I gave Samantha a blow-by-blow account of the Mathletes meet. When I told her some of the problems, she was amazed we could answer them at all.

My jitters were quickly disappearing.

How was dinner? Wonderful. We sat by a window and watched the snow, and I felt as if we'd been transported to the nineteenth century.

While coffee was being served, Dad pulled three tickets out of his jacket pocket with a dramatic flourish. "Anyone interested in seeing *Shooting Star*?"

My mouth hung open. (Don't worry, I'd swallowed.) *Shooting Star* was only the hottest show on Broadway.

"You're kidding!" I said.

"How did you get tickets?" Samantha asked.

"Through my old company. I put the order in before I was downsized." Dad chuckled and looked at his watch. "I figured that after the show we'd take a spin around the city and look at the skyline, then take in some jazz in the Village. I'll show you NYU, where I went to school."

"A nice, relaxed evening," Samantha said with a smile.

"Since we're driving," Dad went on, "it won't take long to — " Suddenly his face went slack. "Oh, no! The car!"

He slapped his credit card on the table. "Give this to the waiter. I'll be right back." With that, he stood up and bolted out the door.

Samantha and I chatted a little tensely until Dad returned, red-faced and holding a parking ticket. "Forty dollars!" he muttered as he sat down. "What an outrage!"

Samantha put her arm around him. "Much cheaper than a garage, huh?"

Dad was a good sport. He tried to laugh about it. But as we walked to the car, I could see him glancing nervously at the windshield, hoping no other ticket had been tucked under the wipers.

We hit major traffic going down Broadway. This did not help Dad's mood one bit. Plus, every single one of the streets was plastered with No Parking signs. No meters in sight. At eight o'clock, curtain time, we were stuck behind a tour bus on West Forty-third Street. "You two go ahead," Dad grumbled. "I'll find a parking garage."

Well, *Shooting Star* was fabulous. I think Dad would have agreed too, except he didn't see all of it. He arrived at the theater just as the first musical number was ending. And he was in such a deep funk, I don't think he noticed much until the second act.

Oh, well, the night was still young.

Unfortunately, it grew old fast as we waited for the garage attendant to retrieve Dad's car. Which now had a thin, foot-long scrape on the passenger side.

"You'll be hearing from my insurance company!" was the last thing Dad said to the attendant as we drove away.

His mood picked up as we drove to the Village, chatting about the show. We even found a legal parking space.

The jazz quartet was wonderful, but Dad whisked us away after two numbers for our tour of NYU.

How was that? Fine, if you adore looking at cement and brick. Every time I spotted some cool-looking store nearby, Dad's reaction would always be something like, "Let me show you where I studied American history."

We ended up at an Italian pastry shop, where Dad and Samantha sipped romantically at their cappuccinos while I tried not to fall asleep in my fruit-sweetened sherbet.

The rest of the night is a blur. I remember Dad's hubcaps were missing when we returned to the car. I remember an argument with a delivery truck driver when we were stopped at a light. And I remember dropping off Samantha at an East Side high-rise building and then circling around Dad's block about twenty times looking for a parking space.

Somehow I managed to stay awake enough to climb the stairs of Dad's building. When we entered his apartment, I noticed the mantel clock read 1:17.

"Wow, what a night, huh?" Dad said. "Let's get some sleep, and I'll drive you back tomorrow. Maybe we can see a movie — "

"I have a baby-sitting job tomorrow," I said with a yawn.

"No problem. I'll stay over at the Strathmore. Maybe we can squeeze in the movie after school Monday."

"Mathletes session," I explained. "And a Baby-sitters Club meeting."

Dad shrugged. "Well, you know me. I have time. How about Tuesday?"

My eyes were closing. "Listen, Dad, I'm tired. Maybe we ought to talk about this tomorrow."

"Sure, sweetheart," Dad replied. "You go ahead and use the bathroom first."

As I shuffled away, visions of sugarless plums danced in my head. It was nice to be with Dad but not exactly relaxing. He was leading his life as if it were one big datebook. And all the appointments in it read STACEY.

CHAPTER 8

Ms. Hartley had a word for our team — juggernaut. When she first said it, I pictured a gallon of milk floating in outer space. But it means something totally different: a powerful force that crushes everything in its way.

A week after our Stoneybrook victory, we competed for the regional championship. Our opponents were two area schools, Howard Township and Mercer. Howard had an amazing captain named Alan Bardwell who had actually taken the math SAT and done well on it — yes, in eighth grade!

I thought I was going to faint before the meet. The crowd at Mercer Middle School was even bigger than the one at SDS. Kristy was leading cheers and being booed by people from the other schools. The pressure was horrible. But Ms. Hartley came to the rescue. She gathered us backstage to do "Zoo Crew." It's a great exercise she said she'd learned in acting class years ago. You ask yourself what kind of animal you feel like. Then you act it out.

I thought, NFM (Not For Me). Nerd City.

Beside me, Bea became a screaming monkey. Jason ran around in circles, bellowing like an elephant. Mari became a yapping Chihuahua.

I felt like laughing. So I became a hyena.

We were hopping around like fools. Kids from the other teams were staring at us in disbelief. But you know what? It felt fantastic.

And my stage fright disappeared.

We ended the meet with 69 points to Howard's 63 and Mercer's 58! (As Ms. Hartley noted, "Howard may have Alan Bardwell, but we have *balance*.")

By the way, I, Stacey the Juggernaut, had a perfect score.

One nice thing about our victories was the publicity. Our regional trophy was put front and center of the SMS trophy case, and a big poster advertised the Southern Connecticut district championship, which was the following Saturday.

This time, a whole bunch of our charges came, including the entire Pike family and the Barrett/DeWitts. It felt like a football game.

The meet was in a gymnasium in Chatham

Middle School. The place smelled like sweat. *Très* noisy, too. When we did Zoo Crew, hardly anyone noticed.

One of our opponents was Saltonstall Prep, whose team members all dressed in jackets and ties. The Chatham team was in normal clothes, but it was equally smart.

On the first question, when each team had a perfect score, I knew we were in trouble.

The lead changed about a dozen times. By the last problem, Saltonstall had 70 points, Chatham had 66, and we had 65.

As one of the Saltonstall members spun the wheel, perspiration dripped down my forehead. Beside me, Emily was shaking.

"I'm hot," Jason whispered.

"Use the showers," I suggested.

"Ha ha."

No one was in a jolly mood just then.

The category was factors and divisibility. The head of Chatham math, Ms. Crandall, read the problem:

"At a Mathletes meet, Mark said to Rebecca, 'I have three siblings. The product of their ages is thirty-six. The sum of their ages is the same as my age. How old are they?' Rebecca thought about that for awhile, then said to Mark, 'Yo! You didn't give me enough information to solve the problem.' Mark apologized and said, 'The oldest one likes rainforest crunch ice cream.' "

Ms. Crandall placed the problem on the overhead projector. We all looked at it with a big group Duh.

"We're sunk," Alexander muttered.

"What does ice cream have to do with it?" Rick asked.

Stacey's First Rule of Math popped into my mind: If in doubt, write.

I grabbed a pencil and said, "Okay, start at the top. What three numbers multiply out to thirty-six?"

"One times one times thirty-six," Bea said.

"One times two times eighteen," Jason added.

I scribbled on and on:

1	1	36
1	2	18
1	3	12
1	4	9
1	6	6
2	2	9
2	3	6
3	3	4

"Now, the sum of the ages has to equal Mark's age," I went on. "So let's add them up."

I inserted plus signs and made sums:

$$1 + 1 + 36 = 38$$
$$1 + 2 + 18 = 21$$
$$1 + 3 + 12 = 16$$
$$1 + 4 + 9 = 14$$
$$1 + 6 + 6 = 13$$
$$2 + 2 + 9 = 13$$
$$2 + 3 + 6 = 11$$
$$3 + 3 + 4 = 10$$

"Now what?" Mari said. "We still don't know Mark's age!"

"I guess fourteen," Jason volunteered.

"You can't *guess*," Bea said. "Rebecca didn't have enough information to solve the problem. That must be a clue."

Bing! A light went on in my head. "She couldn't tell, because two different combinations add up to thirteen! Mark must be thirteen!"

"So how old are the siblings?" Mari asked.

" 'The oldest one likes rainforest crunch'?" Jason read. "What's that supposed to mean?"

I looked at the two "thirteen" sums carefully. Then it hit me. "That's it! His siblings can't be one, six, and six, because there wouldn't be an oldest one. The oldest would be twins!"

I rang the bell and shouted out: "Two, two, and nine!"

"That's correct!" Ms. Crandall replied. "Stoneybrook Middle School wins!"

The gym erupted. It was pandemonium. Chaos. Worse than the World Series.

Well, maybe not that bad. But our team was mobbed. The Pike kids were jumping all around me. Kristy was punching the air and whooping. Mom and Dad actually smiled at each other.

Ms. Hartley gave me a huge hug. "Congratulations, Stacey, you were sensational!"

"Thanks," I said.

"We're going to be in the state finals! I've been dreaming of this for years."

Hoo boy.

State finals. I was going to have to go through all this again.

Claudia rode back to Stoneybrook with me in Dad's car. We needed to drop her off for a tutoring session with Lindsey "I Hate Math" DeWitt. (The Barrett/DeWitts had gone to the meet in one big, overcrowded minivan, which was why Claudia was with us.)

Claud and I sat in the backseat, yakking excitedly about the meet, while Mom and Dad sat silently up front.

You may be wondering what Dad had been up to the previous two weeks. No, he had not found a job yet. Yes, he had been looking. Just about every evening, though, he'd driven out to Stoneybrook. Once Dad even brought Samantha. I thought Mom would freak. She didn't. (Okay, she wasn't doing cartwheels, but she managed to be friendly and polite.)

"Stacey, I am so glad Lindsey went to the meet," Claudia said to me as Mom and Dad remained quiet. "She had a great time. She finally saw how much fun math could be. I mean, it's fun the way *I* do it, but she still hates it in school."

"She may always hate it," I said. "Some kids just do."

"I have a plan. Stoneybrook Elementary is having its math fair next week. A lot of our charges are joining up, even Buddy. Of course, he started teasing Lindsey about it, saying she was too stupid to join, typical stuff. She insisted she could do a math fair project, too, if she wanted to." Claudia smiled. "I think I can convince her to do it."

"She must have really changed," I remarked.

Claudia shrugged. "See for yourself. Come with me to the session."

It didn't sound like a bad idea. I missed seeing Lindsey. Dad had offered to take me to a celebration dinner, but that wouldn't start for a few hours. I asked Dad to drop me off with Claudia.

As we entered the house, Claudia cried out, "Here she is, Stacey the Genius!"

"Clau-*aud!*" I said.

The whole family rushed in. Everyone wanted to talk about the meet.

"Lindsey told us she wants to be like you when she grows up," Franklin announced.

"You set a great example," Mrs. DeWitt chimed in. She turned to Claudia. "Having a terrific tutor doesn't hurt, either."

"How did you know all that stuff, Stacey?" Buddy asked. "I couldn't answer any of those problems."

"She has a brain," Lindsey said. "Unlike you."

"So funny I forgot to laugh," Buddy snapped.

"I saw a mouse under the bleachers," Madeleine claimed.

Mrs. DeWitt looked horrified. "You *did?*"

"It was just a ball of dust," Taylor said.

"Well, the dust walked and had a tail," Madeleine insisted.

Eventually we changed the subject (thank goodness). Claudia, Lindsey, and I went upstairs.

The last time I'd tutored Lindsey, it had taken about a half hour just to convince her to open up her math book. This time she plopped it open on her desk. "I'm learning my times tables," she announced.

"Quick," Claudia said. "What's three times four?"

Lindsey scrunched up her face and began counting on her fingers. "Three plus three is . . . six," she muttered. "Then seven eight nine . . . then ten eleven twelve. Twelve!"

Claudia applauded. "Yeaaaa! Okay, here's a hard one. Six times four."

It took Lindsey a loooong time counting out this one. Finally she said, "Twenty-three?"

I shook my head. "You really should — "

"Off by one, Lindsey," Claudia interrupted.

"Twenty-four!" Lindsey shouted with a big grin.

"Yyyyyyes!" Claudia exclaimed. "Isn't she great?"

"You know, you'd be better off memorizing the tables one at a time," I suggested. "Hold the table in front of you, covering up the answers to test yourself. That way, you can see a pattern while using rote memorization."

"But my way works," Lindsey protested.

"Stacey, she's just starting," Claudia said.

I nodded. "Yes, but you have to start right."

"Lindsey, let's do some borrowing," Claudia suggested, opening Lindsey's book to a page of subtraction problems.

Lindsey worked hard, then showed me what she'd written:

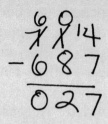

"See," Lindsey explained. "You can't take seven from four, so you borrow a one — "

"Actually, you're borrowing a ten," I explained. "Don't forget, you're taking it from the tens column."

Lindsey looked confused. "Am I supposed to write a ten next to the four?"

"Staceyyyy, you're just being technical," Claudia complained.

"It's not technical at all," I said. "Place value is important. Also, you don't need to write that zero in the hundreds column of the answer. Zeroes are only needed to hold place value if the next highest column is a positive integer."

Lindsey cast a nervous glance at Claudia.

"Well, yeah, Stacey's right about the zero, I guess," Claudia mumbled.

"Can I play downstairs?" Lindsey asked.

"Let's do another problem," Claudia suggested.

Lindsey shook her head. "I'm done."

She bolted from her chair and ran for the door.

"Lindsey?" Claudia called. "Let's do our song for Stacey."

Lindsey thumped downstairs. Claudia thumped after her.

I stayed in the room, feeling like a total dork.

Why couldn't I have shut my mouth? Claudia may not have taught Lindsey the best way, but she'd done a good job. I'd never seen Lindsey so interested in math — until I'd butted in.

I slumped onto the bed. My eyelids felt heavy all of a sudden. I had the urge to curl up and sleep.

Maybe that's why I was so picky with Lindsey. Maybe I was just too tired. All the Mathletes pressure, all the crazy late-night activities with Dad. I needed a normal life again.

Besides, I hadn't baby-sat in awhile. I'd lost touch with all my charges. I knew that if I'd stayed with tutoring, I'd have figured out how to reach Lindsey by now. I wouldn't scare her off.

I thought about quitting Mathletes. But that didn't make sense. Not before the state championship play-offs. The meets were going to take place on Saturday, Monday, and Tuesday. In a little more than a week, I'd be done. Back to baby-sitting. Back to my life.

Well, sort of. Less time with Mathletes meant more time for Dad to plan. More shows and dinners and outings. More tension with Mom.

Hey, ease up, McGill.

For someone whose life was so full, I was feeling pretty sorry for myself.

Maybe I just needed a good night's sleep.

CHAPTER 9

Okay, Problem One:

Mallory Pike is baby-sitting for her seven brothers and sisters. Two of them want to join the Stoneybrook Elementary School math fair. One isn't sure. Three others would rather eat swamp grass on stale bread. The youngest does not qualify but thinks she does and pretends to join. If Mallory is driven out of her mind by them, how many Pikes will be at the math fair, and what will their ages be?

You have three minutes in which to answer.

"Two and two are four . . ." Claire Pike sang the tune of the "Inchworm" song from the movie *Hans Christian Andersen*. "Four and four are eight . . ."

"Will you stop?" said Margo Pike. "We know already!"

"I'm practicing for the math fair!" Claire insisted.

"The math fair is for second grade and up!" Nicky Pike cried.

"No fair," said Claire, storming away.

Claire is the youngest Pike kid. She's five. Margo, who's seven, is the next youngest, then Nicky (eight), Vanessa (nine), and the ten-year-old triplets: Byron, Jordan, and Adam.

Math fever was in the air at Mallory's house. The Pike kids had really enjoyed the Mathletes meet. Claire had been begging Mal to get my autograph (ahem).

Already Margo and Vanessa had signed up for the SES math fair. Nicky was thinking about it. On Sunday, while Mallory was sitting for them all, the girls had decided to start preparing.

Vanessa was hunched over a sheet of paper at the kitchen table. "Da one da two da three da four da five da six da seven."

The triplets were cracking up. "And over here, ladies and gentlemen," Adam said, "is

Vanessa Pike's fascinating experiment —
counting how many times she can say 'Duh'
in one sentence."

"For your information, I'm counting how
many beats are in a line of poetry," Vanessa in-
formed him. "Poems are very mathematical."

"Especially yours," Jordan said. "They multiply, like cockroaches."

"Malloryyyyy!" Vanessa complained.

"Guys," Mallory said, "leave Vanessa alone,
especially if you're not going to enter the fair."

"Chickens," Vanessa taunted.

Byron grabbed a cereal box from the cup-
board and dug both hands in. "I have a great
project. If I have two fistfuls of Cap'n Crunch,
and I eat one . . ." He stuffed his mouth.
"Rmmmmppffrrorrrsshh."

"Eeeww!" Vanessa screamed.

"Byron, you are such a pig," Margo said.

Giggling, the triplets ran away. Vanessa
went back to her poetry.

Next to her, Margo had been busily stacking
coins into piles. She picked up a dollar bill and
ripped it in half.

Vanessa's jaw dropped. "Margo, what are
you doing?"

"I'm showing different ways you can make
fifty cents. See, it's this many pennies — "

"What Vanessa means," Mallory said, "is
that you're not supposed to rip a dollar bill."

"It's against the law!" Vanessa said.

Margo looked horrified. "It is? Am I going to be arrested?"

"RRRRRRRRRRR . . ." wailed Jordan like a police siren, from inside the family room.

"STO-O-O-O-OP!" Margo cried.

"Margo, you won't be arrested," Mallory assured her. "I'll tape it back together, okay?"

From the bathroom, Mallory heard Claire squeal with hysterical laughter.

"Close the door!" Nicky's voice shouted.

Then, "Ooooooooooh, Nicky, you're in big trouble!" from Adam.

Mallory didn't like the sound of this. She ran inside to see Adam pushing against the bathroom door. "What happened?" she asked.

"Nicky's playing with the toilet paper," Adam explained.

"Am not *playing!*" Nicky replied from behind the door.

"Open up," Mallory commanded, elbowing Adam away.

The door creaked slowly open. Nicky was standing in the middle of a huge pile of unrolled toilet paper. His face was red with anger. "You made me lose count, Adam!"

All the Pike siblings were peering inside, screaming with laughter. "You're not supposed to pull so hard!" Byron said.

"This is my math fair project!" Nicky insisted.

That just made the kids howl even louder. "What's it called, arithmetoilet?" Vanessa said.

"Your project is counting toilet paper sheets?" Mallory asked.

"No, it's about estimation," Nicky replied. "I estimate how many sheets are in the roll. Then I count to see if I was right. I'm going to do the same thing with paper towels and raisins in raisin bran — stuff like that. But now, because of stupid Adam, I have to start all over again!"

"The toilet paper package tells you how many sheets are in a roll," Mallory patiently said.

"Oh," Nicky replied.

"Yeah, birdbrain," Adam said.

"*You* didn't know that, Adam," Nicky retorted.

"And what did you plan to do after you finished?" Mallory asked.

"Roll it back up, I guess," Nicky said with a shrug.

Mallory sighed. "Go ahead. Just finish before Mom and Dad come home."

Margo and Vanessa returned to the kitchen, and the triplets ran upstairs to their room. Claire was now staring into the bathroom with a solemn expression. "Um, Mallory?" she said, tugging on Mal's sleeve. "I have to go."

Mallory grabbed her hand. "Come on, I'll take you upstairs."

As they raced through the house, Byron's voice boomed out, *"Hey! What happened to all my quarters?"*

"I'll give them back," Margo called out.

"Whaaaaat?" Byron bolted from his room and nearly collided with Mallory and Claire, who were climbing the stairs.

As Claire sprinted off to the upstairs bathroom, Mallory raced downstairs to break up the war of the coins.

Oh, well, no one ever said math was easy.

CHAPTER 10

*R*rrring!

When the phone rang on Friday morning, I was in the middle of a wrestling match. With my hair.

I was staring in the mirror. Overnight, to my horror, my hair had taken on a life of its own. It was knotted like a den of snakes on one side. On the other, it was levitating upward like a magic carpet.

I glanced at my clock. It was already five minutes past the usual time I go downstairs for breakfast. Well, I didn't care. I was not going to be a bad-hair victim.

I yanked hard with my brush.

"Yeeow!" I cried.

"Stacey, it's your dad!" Mom called from downstairs.

Arrgh. Leave it to Dad to call at a moment like this.

Desperate hair calls for desperate measures. Quickly I pulled apart the knots, brushed my hair out, and yanked it back into a ponytail. Then I dived into Mom's bedroom for the phone.

"Hi," I said. "I have to leave."

Dad chuckled. "That's some way to talk to a loving father who just managed to snag two floor seats to the U4Me concert at Madison Square Garden."

"AAAAAAAAAA!" I screamed. I couldn't help it. It was the first thing that popped into my head.

U4Me's stage show is beyond cool. I saw it once in person, but I didn't really have a chance to appreciate it. The girls I went with were caught with bottles of liquor, and we were all kicked out. (They are *ex*-friends now.)

"Stacey, are you all right?" my mom called from the kitchen.

"Great!" I shouted.

Dad laughed. "When Samantha told her niece I had tickets, she screamed bloody murder. U4Me is her favorite group, too. So, I take it you want to go?"

"*Do* I? How did you get tickets? I heard the concert was sold out."

"From the personnel director of a major

Manhattan company with a fifty-third-floor office, which just may offer me a job as executive vice president!"

"*You got a job?* Congratulations!"

"Whoa, not yet. They're still considering someone else, but my chances are good."

"You'll get it. I know you will."

"I'll tell you more about it after school. I'm picking you up. I figure, if we're going to a concert tomorrow, that doesn't leave much time to buy you a new outfit."

I laughed. "Dad, you are so cool!"

"See you at SMS!"

" 'Bye."

I hung up, grabbed my backpack from my room, and ran downstairs. Too bad I'd combed out my magic carpet hair. I could have climbed on it and flown.

My mom was dressed and ready for work, sipping coffee and reading the newspaper. I poured myself some cereal and milk and began wolfing it down.

"Don't tell me," Mom said. "Your father got a job."

"Not yet." I gulped down a big glob of Rice Krispies. "Guess what? He's taking me to a U4Me concert tomorrow."

Mom looked puzzled. "Oh. I guess it must be an afternoon concert, then?"

CLANG! went a gong in my brain.

The Mathletes meet. I'd been so excited I hadn't even thought of it.

"Oh my lord!" I exclaimed. "It can't conflict. Can it?"

Mom flipped through the entertainment section. "Let's see, the meet's at seven, and the concert . . ."

She opened the paper to a full-page U4Me ad. At the bottom, in large print, it read 8:00 P.M.

My mathematical mind clicked into gear. "Well, if we start right on time, and twelve problems have a three-minute time limit, and the Mathmania problems are answered in an average of two minutes, then we'll be done by — "

Mom was shaking her head. "Forget it, Stacey. The meet is in Hartford. The concert's in New York. That's a two-and-a-half-hour drive. You can't possibly go to the concert. Besides, you've seen U4Me."

"But they have a new CD! And this may be the last big event Dad can take me to before he has a new job."

Mom sighed. "You said he doesn't have it yet. And even if he gets a job, it's not as if he'll drop off the face of the earth."

I looked at the clock and realized I was out of time. "Got to go, Mom."

94

I breakfasted, brushed, and bolted.

At the corner of Elm and Burnt Hill, Claudia and Mary Anne were looking at their watches and waiting.

"Oversleeping or bad hair day?" asked Claudia as I approached.

"Hair," I replied.

Claudia grinned at Mary Anne. "I win."

I ignored the comment. I was too eager to tell them about my concert dilemma.

When I did, Claudia nearly jumped out of her shoes. "Definitely go to the meet. Give me the ticket."

"Uh-uh, no way," I said. "Sorry, Claudia."

"Um, don't you have the state finals?" Mary Anne asked. "As in, all of Connecticut? Do you really want to miss it for a concert?"

"But it's a best-of-three series," I reminded them. "We can still take it if we lose the first game."

"True," Claudia conceded. "Besides, you have Bea the Genius on your team. They are pretty strong without you, Stace. No offense."

"That's not the point, really," Mary Anne said. "I mean, it's a team. Like the BSC. We all show up to meetings. We don't disappear for any old reason."

"That's because Kristy would kill us," Claudia remarked.

"It's not any old reason," I argued. "This is the concert of a lifetime."

Mary Anne shrugged. "I guess."

"My dad went through a lot of trouble to do this," I went on. "And as soon as he has a new job, forget it. I'll never see him."

"Stacey's right," Claudia said. "What's more important, family or math?"

Mary Anne couldn't argue with that.

I had made up my mind.

At lunchtime I heard someone listening to a U4Me CD on a Sony Discman. During English class my teacher caught Grace Blume reading the autobiography of Skyllo, the band's lead singer.

I took these as signs I was making the right decision.

I did not, however, mention my decision to any of my teammates. I had to tell Ms. Hartley first. And I didn't have the chance to see her until after school.

My teeth were chattering when I walked into her classroom.

Family or math . . .

Family or math . . .

I kept repeating Claudia's words to myself.

Ms. Hartley broke into a huge smile when she saw me. "Heyyy, it's the math champ of Connecticut! I have something I need to show you."

As she rooted around in her desk, I blurted out, "Ms. Hartley, I have some bad news."

Ms. Hartley glanced up from her desk, holding a computer printout. Her smile had vanished. "Are you all right?"

"I'm fine. It's just that — well, you see — " *Say it, McGill!* my brain commanded. "I won't be able to make the meet tomorrow."

There. Done. It was off my chest.

Ms. Hartley looked at me blankly, as if I'd just recited something in Icelandic.

"It's — it's because — well, it's a family thing," I stammered. "With my dad."

"Oh. I see." Ms. Hartley nodded grimly. "Well, I — I hope everything works out. This is a disappointment. We'll certainly miss you."

"But I'll be able to make the other two meets," I added. "Or one. I mean, if we win the first and we only need one to win two. I wouldn't miss those . . . or *that*."

Ugh. I needed to stop while I was ahead.

"I understand, Stacey," Ms. Hartley said. "Really. Sorry if I seem preoccupied. It's just that Bea has come down with strep throat. She's contagious for twenty-four hours, so she won't be at the meet, either."

I felt as if someone had just conked me over the head with a baseball bat.

"Oh, no," I murmured. "Well, maybe I can ask — "

"You have to do what you have to do," Ms. Hartley said, forcing a smile. "We'll be fine. We still have seven strong players."

A picture flashed through my mind. The entire SMS Mathletes team, sitting dejectedly in the middle of a huge stadium. Balloons and confetti filling the air. One side of the bleachers screaming. The other side sobbing, as a deep voice blares out, "Stoneybrook . . . zero!"

And where was I in this picture? Miles away, bouncing along to U4Me. A traitor to my team. Like Nero, fiddling while Rome burned.

Was I nuts?

I had to change my plans before it was too late.

"Ms. Hartley — " I began.

"Oh, I never showed you this!" she interrupted, handing me the computer printout. "The individual scoring totals of every Mathlete in the state — and look who's tied for number one!"

The sheet contained a long list of names and numbers in tiny print. But the top one jumped out at me:

Yes, that's me. (The *A* stands for my full name, Anastasia.) Just below my name, it said SINGH, G., with the same score.

"Apparently, George Singh is a real hotshot in Eastbury," Ms. Hartley explained. "You'll meet him in the finals. Newspaper articles have been written about him. So you can be quite proud of yourself."

Proud? I was flabbergasted! Me, little unknown Stacey, number one in the state?

No, *tied* for number one. Which meant I could become number one.

That is, unless I skipped a meet for a concert.

Boy, did I feel like a doofus.

"Ms. Hartley," I tried again, "you know, I may be able to — "

"Excuse me?" a voice piped up. "Stacey?"

I turned to see one of the teacher's aides, Ms. Kolinsky, in the doorway.

"I was told you might be here," she continued. "Your dad is here. He was wondering if — "

"There she is!" said Dad, walking into the room.

I swallowed my words.

Great. This was just what I needed. A big scene with Dad. He'd mention the concert, and Ms. Hartley would know the reason I'd turned my back on my teammates.

Ms. Hartley stood up and extended her hand. "Mr. McGill, may I be the first to congratulate you on your daughter's great success!"

The two of them could not stop oohing and ahhing about my score. As we walked toward the front lobby, all I could manage were a few smiles and thank yous.

With a quick good-bye, Ms. Hartley ducked into the office. Dad and I headed outside.

"So, where will it be?" Dad asked. "Steven E? Bellair's? Zingy's? You name it! Oh, I know what you're going to say. Don't worry. I called Mom and she said it was okay. And I promise to drive you back in time for your Baby-sitters Club meeting. So, you name the store."

I thought about protesting, but I couldn't. Dad would be heartbroken.

Boy, had I blown it. I was stuck.

I should have been thrilled. I was about to buy a new outfit. I was going to see my favorite rock group of all time. All out of the generosity of my dad. I tried to feel cheery.

"Zingy's, I guess," I muttered.

"Don't sound so happy," Dad said with a teasing smile.

I smiled back. I was absolutely miserable.

CHAPTER 11

"IIIII ammm zee famoose Madammm Math!" intoned Haley Braddock, from behind a black veil. "My asseestant, the Duke of Digits, shall make words appear magically from nommmm-bairs!"

Haley's younger brother, Matt, fished some magnetic letters out of a hat and put them on the Johanssens' refrigerator:

01134

"Moomba lazoooomba!" Haley chanted.

Matt turned around the numbers so they looked like this:

HELLO

"Moomba lazoooomba?" Charlotte Johanssen burst out giggling. She was wearing a veil made of taped-together tissues, and they fell off her head. "This is dumb."

"No, it's great," Haley insisted. "Everyone else at the math fair will be doing boring stuff. You know, like 'Remainders and me.' 'Fun with times tables.' But when people see our poster — Madam Math and Countess Countsworthy — they'll say, *'That's* original!' "

Matt glared at her and began communicating in sign language. (He's profoundly deaf, which means he hears absolutely no sound.)

Haley wearily signed back. "Okay, the Duke can be on the poster, too."

It was Saturday morning, and I was baby-sitting for Charlotte Johanssen. Mary Anne was taking care of Haley and Matt. Since all three kids planned to be in the SES math fair, I had suggested we get them together.

Usually sitting for Char puts me in a good mood. She and I are very close. We call each other almost-sisters. She's quiet and thoughtful and very bright.

That Saturday, however, I was a train wreck.

I had not slept well. I'd had a recurring nightmare: I was in Madison Square Garden, wearing my brand-new outfit, bought at a fabulous discount at Zingy's. I was clapping rhythmically, waiting for U4Me to emerge. The arena went dark, the crowd screamed with anticipation, and when the lights blinked on, the stage was filled with . . . Connecticut's top Mathletes teams!

Do I sound a little guilty?

I was.

I kept thinking of the look on Ms. Hartley's face when I told her I was skipping the event.

Why couldn't I just have spoken up? Why couldn't I just have said, "You're right, Ms. Hartley. See you Saturday night"?

I knew why.

Because if I had, I'd be guilty about the expression on *Dad's* face.

Arrghh!

"Don't you guys think it's a good idea?" Haley was asking.

"I think it's great," Mary Anne said.

"Mm-hm," I agreed.

I tried to look enthusiastic. After all, I was the current-but-soon-to-be-ex math champ of the entire state. I was a role model.

A *roll* model was more like it. I felt as if I'd been rolled over.

" 'And now, the magic repeating numbers,' " Charlotte read from a looseleaf sheet.

" 'Zee magic rrrrepeateeng nommmbairs,' " Haley corrected her, rolling the *r*'s.

" 'Geeeve me a nommmbair from one to ten

and I weel make it repeat three times,' " Charlotte read aloud, trying to imitate Haley's accent..

"Mootch better," said Madame Math. "Go ahead, Mary Anne."

"Seven," Mary Anne said.

"Moomba lazoomba," Charlotte said, fighting back a laugh. She took a marker and wrote 7. Then she said, "First I weel mooltiply it by 37 . . ."

She did, and she wrote the answer: 259.

"Goodness, zat ees not a reepeating seven! What shall I do?" (Countess Countsworthy was really warming up now.) "Hmmm, let me mooltiply zees by three."

With a flourish, Charlotte wrote 259 x 3 = 777.

"Yes!" she crowed. "I have made zee seven repeat!"

Mary Anne and I applauded.

"That's fantastic," Mary Anne said.

Personally, I love repeating-number tricks. Our team had worked on them in practice. "You know," I said, "you can stretch that trick to six digits instead of three."

"Cool," Haley said. "I mean, vonnnderfool."

I took a pen and began writing. "You see, here's how you made Mary Anne's number repeat. Basically, you did this . . .

$$7 \times \underline{111} = 777$$

"But you broke down that one hundred eleven into two factors, three and thirty seven . . .

$$7 \times \underline{3} \times \underline{37} = 777$$

"To make the trick look more complex, you split the problem into two parts . . ."

$$7 \times \underline{37} = 259$$
$$259 \times \underline{3} = 777$$

Oops.

I was going overboard. I knew it. Mary Anne's eyes were glazing over. Charlotte and Haley were staring at the paper. All I could think about was Lindsey, about how I almost ruined her math skills for life.

I wasn't going to do it again. I was not going to complicate anything. Let the kids discover math for themselves.

I put the pencil down. "So, uh, anyway, your trick is great just the way it is."

"What's the other trick?" Haley asked.

"It's nothing," I replied. "Do another one you planned."

"Hey, that's not fair!" Charlotte complained.

Haley was signing something to Matt. Immediately he picked up the pencil and scribbled 111,111 on the paper.

"All riiight, Matt!" Mary Anne said. "Multiplying, in second grade!"

"He just knows the ones table," Haley replied. "I taught it to him."

"Okay, so you multiply the number by 111, 111, and it repeats six times," Charlotte said. "What's the trick, Stacey?"

"It's really for older kids," I explained.

Charlotte frowned. "We're both above grade level."

Matt and Haley were signing again. "Matt says you multiply littler numbers," Haley said. "Same as last time."

"Well, he has the right idea," I began.

The three kids were staring at me. They looked so eager. I was dying to explain the trick.

I took a deep breath and picked up the pencil. If they fell asleep from boredom, I could always tuck them in for a nap.

"Okay, let's see how the number breaks down . . .

$$111,111 = 111 \times 1001$$

"We know that one hundred eleven breaks down into factors — and so does one thousand and one!"

$$111,111 = 111 \times 1001$$
$$\underline{3} \times \underline{37} \times \underline{7} \times \underline{11} \times \underline{13}$$

"So if we take a number, like five," Haley said, "and multiply it by all those little numbers you underlined, in any order — "

"We'll get five five five five five five!" Charlotte exclaimed.

"Try it," I said.

Well, the multiplication was very hard for both girls. Mary Anne and I had to help them. But when they got the answer, 555,555, they were ecstatic.

"That is so cool!" Charlotte said. "Can we make the number repeat nine times?"

I shrugged. "Let's figure it out."

Charlotte ran upstairs and brought back a calculator. We all huddled around it and tried to find the factors of 111,111,111.

We got as far as 3 x 3 x 37 x 333,667 before we gave up.

Countess Countsworthy practically tackled her parents when they returned home. She, Madam Math, and the Duke of Digits insisted on performing a preview in the living room.

The reaction? "Stacey, you live up to your reputation," Dr. Johanssen said. (Boy, did that ever feel good.)

"Can we go to see Stacey in the Mathletes championship later?" Charlotte asked. "Please?"

"I suppose," Dr. Johanssen said. "Where is it?"

"Well, actually, I'm not competing today," I replied. "I, uh, have another appointment."

"To do what?" Charlotte asked.

"See a concert," I muttered.

"For *that* you're going to miss the championships?" Haley asked.

Mr. Johanssen chuckled. "I'm sure the team is saying the same thing."

Zing. Did I feel guilty again.

We said our good-byes, and I walked with Mary Anne back to the Braddocks'. After dropping off Matt and Haley, we headed along Elm Street.

I barely said a word. My thoughts were like passengers on the New York subway, crowded and bumping into each other.

"Mary Anne," I said. "Did I blow it or what?"

"No way," Mary Anne answered. "I think the kids had a great time!"

"No, I mean the meet."

"Oh, that." Mary Anne suddenly looked concerned. "Are you changing your mind?"

I took a deep breath. The words just spilled out. "My team needs me, Mary Anne. They may become state champs. Yesterday Ms. Hartley told me I'm tied for the state individual scoring record. I mean, I must be crazy. I've worked so hard, I've had a good time, and now, just when they need me the most, I'm gone."

"Remember what you said, Stacey — family over math."

"*Claudia* said that. My dad went through so much trouble. He's trying so hard to spend time with me. I want him to know I appreciate him. And I do want to see U4Me. Sort of. I mean, this is my second time. . . ."

"Sounds like you really don't want to go."

"I don't!"

"So tell your dad. He'll understand. What's the worst that could happen? He'll dock your allowance until you pay for the ticket?"

"He doesn't give me an allowance."

"Stacey, did your dad ask you beforehand if you wanted those tickets?"

"No. That's not his style. He usually doesn't ask. He just kind of *announces*. It drives my mom crazy."

"What does he do when she says no?"

I shrugged. "Apologizes, I guess."

"Then you don't have to worry. Tell him everything you told me. He'll understand. Stacey, you have a whole lifetime to do stuff with your dad. There will always be rock concerts. But there's only one state championship this year."

I had to admit, Mary Anne was right.

I knew just what to do.

CHAPTER 12

"What do you mean, give the tickets to Samantha's niece?" Dad asked over the phone.

"It's what she wants, right?" I said. "She'll love you for it."

"But I thought you and I — "

"Please don't be mad, Dad. When you first told me, I was so excited that I wasn't thinking. I didn't realize I'd be missing the state championship — "

"Whoa, hold it," Dad said. "That's at the same time?"

"Didn't you know?"

"No! I mean, I wasn't really connecting. I mean — "

I couldn't help laughing. "You're as bad as me!"

"You can't miss a championship meet!"

"That's what I say."

"Does Mom know about this?" Dad asked.

"Yup."

Did she ever. I had talked this out with her the moment I arrived home. Now she was standing by the phone, giving me moral support.

"Okay, look, Stacey. You don't have much time. But don't rush. Eat a good dinner. The tickets are at the box office. I'll call Samantha, then I'll leave from here at the Strathmore and meet you in Hartford. Make sure to take I-95 . . ."

As Dad rambled on, I gave Mom the high sign.

We were in business.

I hung up at 5:07. The meet was at seven o'clock, and we had a long drive ahead of us.

I tapped out Ms. Hartley's number on the phone and heard an answering machine message. "Hi, this is Stacey," I said breathlessly. "If you're checking in for messages, I'm coming!"

We left the house at 5:33. I don't even remember what we ate for dinner. I must have gobbled it down, though, because my stomach hurt like crazy in the car.

Of course, it may have been Mom's driving.

Now, I love my mom dearly, but being in a car with her is like riding a bull. Around New Haven, I thought I was going to lose my dinner. Outside Wallingford, we hit a traffic jam. I almost hopped out and ran.

We arrived at the Eastbury Middle School parking lot at 7:02. I pushed the car door open so hard I nearly fell onto the asphalt.

"Go ahead!" Mom said. "Let them know you're here!"

I sprinted into the school through a side entrance. I could hear a huge cheer from behind closed gym doors at the end of a hall. I burst through and yelled, "I'm here!"

A couple of sweaty guys on a rubber mat looked up at me briefly and then started pummeling each other.

A wrestling match. Wrong doors.

"Where's the Mathletes meet?" I asked a teenage boy who was standing on the sidelines.

"Auditorium." He pointed into the hallway. "Right, right, left."

I went right, right, left. I ran smack into a wall of people.

"Mathletes?" I asked a gray-haired man.

"Sorry, it's at capacity," he said. "The AV shop is wiring a closed-circuit TV for us — "

"Excuse me . . . excuse me . . ." I elbowed my way through the crowd. Just inside the auditorium door, a young woman said, "You'll have to wait, miss — "

"*I'm on the Stoneybrook team! Where's Ms. Hartley?*"

I was a total maniac. I think I scared the poor woman out of her shoes.

I didn't wait for her to answer. I could see my team huddled with Ms. Hartley on a huge stage. Jason was looking nervously out at the crowd.

My feet have never moved so fast. I sprinted down the aisle and jumped onto the stage. "Okay, guys," I shouted. "Let's go for it!"

The huddle parted. Seven jaws hit the stage floor at the same time. My teammates looked as if they'd just seen Santa Claus fly in on the back of the Easter Bunny.

"Stacey?" Mari said.

"I could make it — my dad — I didn't really — I'll explain later!" I gasped.

"Will the teams kindly take their seats?" a voice boomed out.

Ms. Hartley was beaming. "SMS Mathletes," she shouted, "are we ready?"

"YYYYYYYESSSSSS!"

The state finals are different from the other meets. Not only is it a best-of-three series, but only two teams are involved.

The table across from us was full of strangers — very smart-looking strangers. I had no idea which one was my rival, George Singh, and I didn't want to know.

My heart was pounding. My brain was snapping.

114

I answered the first few questions practically before I finished reading them.

My teammates were on fire, too. Through the first eight questions, we had a perfect score. Then we lost one to Eastbury, and they took a team question.

Suddenly we were neck and neck. The lead changed hands with just about every question. The meet sped by so fast I can barely remember it.

But I do know for sure that the final score was SMS 75, Eastbury 73.

Afterward, I was mobbed by my teammates. Emily was practically in tears. Rick wouldn't stop shouting in my ears. Jason was riding around on Gordon, piggyback-style.

"Partyyyyy!" Jason shouted.

"Great idea!" Ms. Hartley said. "My treat! How does the Rosebud sound?"

"Yeeaaa!" was the response.

"Check with your parents," Ms. Hartley said. "We'll meet there as close to nine-thirty as possible."

I spotted Mom in one of the aisles, making her way toward me. She looked so proud.

I practically leaped off the stage. We buried each other in hugs and congratulations.

"Can I use your phone card?" I asked. "I promised to call Mary Anne as soon as the meet was over."

Mom fished the card out of her purse. I ran into the hallway, found a pay phone, and tapped out Mary Anne's number.

"Hello?" her voice answered.

"We did it!" I shouted.

Well, Mary Anne screamed so loudly I thought I'd lose my hearing. I gave her the details and then told her about the Rosebud.

"I'll call everyone," Mary Anne said. "We'll meet you there!"

"Great! 'Bye."

" 'Bye."

Back to the auditorium. Now Mom was talking to Dad. He let out a whoop when he saw me.

"Where were you sitting?" I asked.

"I wasn't," he replied. "I was standing in the back. Didn't you hear me shouting? The guy in front almost slugged me. His kid was on the Eastbury team."

"Daa-aad — "

"I didn't care. I'm a father. I have a right to be proud. I say we celebrate!"

"Well, my teammates are all — " I began.

"I am taking all three of us out," Dad barreled on. "That is, if your mom doesn't mind."

Mom was fidgeting. She looked as if she wanted to slug him. "Ed — I don't think this is proper — "

Dad was grinning. "I will not take no for an answer. We've had dinner together at home. We can survive a restaurant. It's a happy day all around. I have some news of my own."

"What news?" I asked.

"I'll tell you at Renwick's. I made a reservation for three."

Mom and I gave each other a Look. Now she seemed curious. I knew just what was running through her mind. The same things that were running through mine:

He's engaged to Samantha.

He found a job.

He's moving to Tibet.

One thing was sure. I could not say no. I could always show up at the Rosebud a little late.

Mom and I followed his car back to Stoneybrook. We listened to the radio and hardly said a word.

At the restaurant, Dad ordered nachos and guacamole. Then, with a big smile on his face, he cleared his throat and announced, "Fifty-third floor. A view of the Hudson River. A very easy subway ride from my apartment."

"You got that great new job!" I exclaimed.

"Congratulations, Ed," Mom said.

"Well, it's not exactly what I dreamed of. The pay is actually lower than my old job, but there's room for advancement. I have to be in

Atlanta on Monday for some intensive meetings with the home office, then I fly back to New York on Tuesday to start work."

"Tuesday?" I said. "Then you'll miss the second meet."

Dad frowned. "Oh. Sorry, Stace. I — I guess, in the excitement of it all — "

"That's okay," I lied. "You can come to the final on Monday. I mean, if it goes to three."

"Well, I'm not sure, sweetheart," Dad said. "I mean, it'll be a weekday, and I'll have a lot of catching up to do."

I nodded. "Well . . . try, okay?"

"Sure," Dad replied. "So, anyway, I get this call from the chief operations officer, who's an old college buddy, and he says, 'Have you heard?' "

I felt as if I'd been kicked. Dad hadn't sounded very disappointed about missing the Monday meet. And how could he even think of skipping the final one?

Now he was rambling on about his job, job, job. His face was lit up, as if he'd just discovered gold.

What happened to New Dad? The caring, "no more workaholic," car-driving dad who had practically moved into the Strathmore just to spend "quality time" with his beloved daughter?

Was my life so unimportant now, just because of a job?

He sounded like the Old Dad to me.

I tried to smile and listen. I tried not to be mad. I tried to understand how important this job was. Important enough to steal me away from the victory celebration with my teammates at the Rosebud.

"Yikes!" I blurted out. "I have to make a call!"

I spotted a telephone by the restrooms. I made a beeline to it and tapped out Mary Anne's number.

"Hello?" answered her father.

"Hi, Mr. Spier, it's Stacey. I — "

"Stacey! You just missed Mary Anne. She called from the Rosebud Cafe. Are you going to be there?"

"I can't go now. If she calls back, would you tell her I'm at Renwick's with my parents? I'll explain another time."

"Will do. Thanks."

" 'Bye."

Ugh. I could picture the Rosebud now. My two sets of friends, all sitting around, not knowing what to say to each other.

All because of my father and his stupid job.

Whoa. Ease up, I told myself. Be mature. Jobs are good. I should be happy. And my friends were not babies. They'll adjust. They'll party together or party separately. Either way they can have a good time. I'll tell them everything later, and they'll understand.

As I headed back to the table, Dad raised a glass. "A toast! To bright futures."

"To bright futures," my mom echoed.

I lifted my glass too. But I didn't say anything. I was afraid of what might come out.

CHAPTER 13

WHAT WE LEARNED ^{sunday}
AT THE SES MATH FAIR
by Abigail Stevenson
and Jessi Ramsey

1. Baby-sitting for 5 Barrett/DeWitt kids isn't any easier than baby-sitting for 7.

2. Don't believe any elementary school fair that claims it's noncompetitive.

3. Even third-graders can make you feel stupid...

"**S**tep right up!" yelled Buddy Barrett. "Can you beat the odds?"

Buddy was standing in front of a small table. On it was a quarter, next to a handwritten report entitled PROBABILTY BY BUDDY BARRETT. (Spelling by Buddy Barrett, too.) Behind him, tacked onto the wall of the SES gym, was a chart that looked like this:

It was Sunday, and the SES math fair was in full gear. Throughout the gym, kids from third to sixth grade had set up booths on long tables. Families milled around, gathering in clumps at the exhibits.

Abby and Jessi were baby-sitting for the younger Barrett/DeWitt kids, while Buddy and Lindsey demonstrated their projects. (Yes, Lindsey. She had insisted on having a booth, with Claudia's help.)

"Buddyyyyyy!" squealed Marnie, clapping and jumping, as if she were seeing her brother on TV.

"You better watch where you leave your change," Abby remarked, pointing to Buddy's quarter.

Buddy rolled his eyes. "You're supposed to flip it and call heads or tails!"

Abby tossed the coin upward. "Tails!"

It landed tails, and Abby whooped. "Yyyyes! What do I win?"

Buddy put a mark in the Tails column. "Nothing. It's probability. You see — fourteen heads, fourteen tails. Just the way I predicted."

"No-o-o-o, Ryan!"

The scream made Abby spin around. Ryan DeWitt was reaching over the top of Lindsey's table. His little paws were toppling over small plastic bowling pins.

Claudia began picking them up, and Abby helped. They placed the pins on circles Lindsey had drawn on a place mat. From above, the pins looked like this:

```
      o
    o  o
  o  o  o
 o  o  o  o
```

The title of Lindsey's booth was Rearrangements: Fun with Geometry.

"This looks cool," Abby said. "Do I get to bowl?"

"No, silly," Lindsey replied. "Rearrange the pins so they point toward you, but you can only move three of them."

Abby chuckled. "Piece of cake!"

"That's what you think," Claudia said.

Abby moved and moved and moved and moved. Five minutes later, Lindsey was practically on the floor laughing. "And you're *thirteen?*"

"I give up!" Abby cried.

Lindsey quickly moved the pins. Here's how:

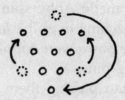

"Come on, Ryan," Abby said, taking his hand. "She's too smart for us."

Lindsey was glowing. (So was Claudia.)

Down the aisle, Vanessa Pike was performing for an audience that included Jessi and Suzi.

Behind Vanessa was a poster entitled Poetry and Number Combinations, with all kinds of number sequences underneath. "Choose from any of these combinations," Vanessa announced, "and see what kind of poetry I can make!"

"That one!" Suzi cried out, pointing to 9–9–6–6–9.

"That's a limerick," Vanessa said. "Each

number tells you how many syllables in a line." She thought a moment, then recited:

"There once was a young girl named Suzi,
Whose pimples were getting all oozy,
One zit was so loaded,
The poor girl exploded,
And that's what became of young Suzi."

Vanessa's audience cracked up. Well, except for Suzi. Her face crumpled.

"It was a joke," Vanessa explained.

Too late.

"Waaaaah!" sobbed Suzi, running away.

Vanessa and Jessi ran after her. They found her hiding behind a pile of wrestling mats.

After a lot of hugging and comforting, they brought Suzi back.

They found Adam, Jordan, and Byron behind Vanessa's table.

"Vanessa Pike loves to do math," Adam chanted, "but we wish she would go take a bath . . ."

"Get out of there!" Vanessa shouted.

Now Suzi was laughing.

As the triplets ran away, giggling, Jessi caught a glimpse of Charlotte, Haley, and Matt — or Madam Math, Countess Countsworthy, and the Duke of Digits. They were sitting behind their table, scowling.

Jessi elbowed Abby. They herded Marnie and Ryan toward the booth.

"How's it going?" Abby asked.

"It's unfair," Haley mumbled.

"Bruce Cominsky's booth stinks," Charlotte said.

Across the aisle, Bruce was setting up an exhibit with the same title as Charlotte and Haley's: NUMBER TRICKS.

"Maybe his tricks are different," Jessi suggested.

Charlotte shook her head. "We checked."

"He doesn't have costumes and cool accents," Abby said.

"We sound dorky," Haley replied.

That was when Jessi spotted me walking through the door. "Stacey!" she yelled.

I ran to her. The girls explained the situation, and I went to work. (Don't worry. I just suggested and hinted. They came up with some new number tricks that were pretty cool. Soon the Madam, the Countess, and the Duke were back in business.)

Next Jessi and Abby visited Margo, who was belting out, "Come visit Margo's Money Madness!"

"Mine is more fun!" Buddy shouted from across the aisle. "Come flip a coin, everybody!"

"That's not even math!" Margo said. "*I* make change. *I* show how much foreign money is worth."

Buddy made a loud snoring noise. "How interesting."

"Truce!" Jessi yelled.

"Toos!" Marnie echoed.

"Doos!" Ryan demanded. (That's his word for *juice*.)

Buddy and Margo started laughing. Jessi went digging around in the diaper bag for Ryan's bottle.

Abby wandered off with Madeleine and Ryan. They found Taylor, ripping off paper towels at Nicky Pike's "Estimation" booth.

"Yo, Taylor, that's part of the exhibit!" Abby warned.

Nicky waved her off. "Doesn't matter. It's a stupid project, anyway."

"Looks pretty good to me," Abby said. "What do I do?"

On Nicky's table were a glass jar full of marbles, a coiled string of Clixx, rolls of various paper products, and a rectangular building made of Legos.

"Just estimate," Nicky mumbled.

Abby eyed the marble jar. "Um . . . five hundred?"

Nicky shook his head. "Uh-uh. Best thing to

do is count the ones on top. Then try to figure out how many layers of marbles there are, top to bottom. Multiply those two numbers."

Abby counted sixteen marbles on top and figured the pile must have been about twelve marbles high. "Let's see . . . I think . . . one hundred ninety-two?"

"Two hundred and one," Nicky said.

"Yeaa!" Abby said. "Great technique, Nicky. This is terrific."

"It stinks," Nicky said, glowering at a nearby booth.

Uh-oh. Another case of low math esteem.

Abby turned to see Sophie McCann and a very professional-looking poster that said MATH AND GENETICS/DOMINANCE AND RECESSIVE-NESS AS PREDICTED BY THE MENDELIAN MODEL. Behind her table were complicated charts, fancy printouts of family trees, and glossy photographs.

Gulp.

"This isn't a competition," Abby said. "You don't need to be jealous of that."

"I *know*," Nicky snapped. "But hers is better."

As Sophie grinned triumphantly at them, a gray-haired man walked up to her. "Ah, I remember Mendelian boxes. So, tell me, what are my chances of having blue eyes if only my maternal grandmother has them?"

Sophie's face reddened. "Well, um, I have to check with my mom," she squeaked. "She's a scientist, and, well, I'm not totally sure, but the charts explain it."

Abby gave Nicky a Look.

"She doesn't know what it means, either!" Nicky whispered. Then, with a big smile on his face, he began shouting, "Impress your friends! Learn how to guess right! Step right this way!"

"Can I guess the toilet paper roll?" Taylor asked.

Abby smiled as a small crowd began to form around Nicky. That was when she noticed Marnie's face reddening. A sudden, unexpected aroma wafted upward.

Jessi approached, crinkling her nose. "Uh-oh, Marnie's involved in a little math project of her own, huh?"

"What's that?" Abby said.

Jessi shrugged. "The process of elimination."

On the way to the rest room, Abby could not stop giggling.

CHAPTER 14

"Good luck, Stacey!"

Claudia gave me a big hug. A bus was rumbling up to the front of SMS, and a small group of kids pressed toward it.

"I wish you guys could come," I said.

Claudia nodded. "Me too. Bad timing, huh?"

It sure was. The second meet was to take place at a "neutral site": an old theater near New Haven, halfway between Eastbury and Stoneybrook. (Originally the meet was supposed to be in the SMS auditorium. But because of snow day postponements, a couple of other groups were using it.) The meet was at an unusual time too — four-thirty. Which meant a lot of parents couldn't attend.

Not to mention students. The only kids boarding the bus were my Mathletes teammates and some of their best friends.

Not mine, of course. The meet was too close

to BSC meeting time. (I'd talked it over with Kristy long ago, and she'd said it was okay for me to miss a meeting.)

No dad, no mom, no BSC. I had to admit, the meet was beginning to feel like an anticlimax.

Plus, I was tired and cranky. I couldn't help noticing that Claudia was the only BSC member who'd bothered to see me off.

Kristy had acted pretty weird around me all weekend. So had the others. Even at the math fair, I felt they'd been avoiding me.

I figured I'd sit with them at lunch on Monday, but Rick Chow had practically pulled me over to the table where the Mathletes were sitting.

"Claudia," I said, "are you guys mad at me?"

"What makes you ask that?"

"I don't know. Ever since Saturday, I've had this funny feeling. You told everyone why I didn't go to the Rosebud, right? The way I explained it to you on the phone?"

Claudia and I had had a long conversation on Saturday night. She'd listened to my complaints about Dad, and she'd promised to let everyone know why I hadn't joined them that night.

"I did explain it," Claudia said.

"Then why are they acting so weird?"

Claudia shrugged. "They were a little annoyed. They'll be okay."

Honnk! Honnnnnk! "Come on, Stacey!" yelled Ms. Hartley from the bus door.

"We'll talk later," I said, running off.

"Good luck!" Claudia called after me.

I could barely concentrate on the trip to Eastbury. What a change from the last meet. My mom was at work. My dad was off in Atlanta, probably too excited even to be thinking of me. And now my best friends were mad at me.

I climbed onto the bus and sat next to Mari. "Hi," she said. "We missed you on Saturday."

"You're annoyed too?" I asked.

"No. I just said we missed you. That's all."

I felt like a jerk. "I'm sorry. It's just that a bunch of my other friends went over to the Rosebud too. And they're not talking to me."

Mari nodded. "I saw them. They didn't look too happy. Kristy Thomas kept snapping at the waiter."

"What did you guys do?"

"We said hi and talked a little. But we couldn't fit any more at our table. Besides, we wanted to be together and talk about the meet."

"So what did my friends do?"

Mari shrugged. "Nothing. They hung out for awhile. Then I looked up and they were gone."

Jason turned around from the seat in front

of us. "Why are you so worried about them?" he asked. "We were the ones you stood up."

"*I didn't stand you up!* I had to go out with my mom and dad. I mean, is that so hard to understand?"

"Touchy, touchy," Jason said.

I hardly said another word all the way to Eastbury.

I don't want to go into all the gory details about the meet. Let's just say it wasn't one of my all-time favorite experiences. For one thing, my stage fright struck again. Looking into an audience of strangers was terrifying. For another, the whole place went crazy every time George Singh scored a point.

Halfway through, I made a stupid mistake on a problem and answered it wrong. You should have heard the cheering. I mean, how rude! I realized then that a lot of people were keeping a running score between George and me. They were waiting for me to fail.

Well, I didn't upset them. I blew the last answer, and Eastbury won, 71–69.

Did my dad call that night from Atlanta to ask about the meet? No. And I didn't know the name of his hotel, so I couldn't call him.

Not that I wanted to. I didn't call anyone. I was feeling pretty miserable. When Claudia phoned me, I told her the score and said I had to go to bed.

The moment I hit the pillow, my eyes sprang open. I was angry at Dad. I was angry at myself for blowing the meet. I was angry at my BSC friends for not being more understanding.

I fell asleep grumpy, and I woke up the next morning even grumpier.

I grumped my way through breakfast, and then I walked grumpishly to the corner to meet Claudia and Mary Anne.

I could tell they'd heard about the meet. They were giving me pitying looks.

As we walked to school, Mary Anne finally said, "I was sorry to hear about last night."

"Me too," Claudia added.

I nodded. "It's okay."

That was it. Neither of them brought the subject up again. When we reached school, Kristy, Abby, Mallory, and Jessi were standing just inside the front door, gabbing.

They stopped when they saw me.

"Hi, Stace," Jessi said quietly.

"I guess you all heard too, huh?" I said.

"We couldn't believe the genius squad actually lost," Abby replied. "What'd they do, slip in a couple of social studies questions to throw you off track?"

I was not in the mood for Abby's humor. "They're not geniuses."

Abby shrugged. "You have to admit, Stacey, they are kind of brainy."

"I couldn't understand half the things they were saying at the Rosebud," Kristy added. "It was like being at a nerd convention."

"I thought they were talking another language," Claudia said.

"Well, they happen to be my friends," I snapped. "And at least *they* understood why I wasn't there that night. Unlike you guys."

"Whoa, Stacey — " Kristy began.

"I didn't ask to go out with my parents, you know. My dad just said we were going. Do you think it's easy having a parent like that? Someone you never see who drops out of the sky and suddenly wants to do stuff with you all the time? What are you supposed to do, say no? None of you knows what that's like. And if you can't get that into your heads, I quit the BSC."

My friends were looking at me as if I'd gone loony.

"Uh, Stacey," Abby said, "one problem. No one's mad at you."

"Yeah," Kristy added. "And I know exactly how you feel about your father — that's the way mine was."

"Then why were you guys so weird at the math fair?" I asked.

"We hardly saw you," Mallory said. "You were helping Charlotte and Haley."

"Some of us were baby-sitting," Abby reminded me.

"You sound angry, Stacey," Mary Anne said softly. "Are you sure you're angry at us?"

I slumped against the wall. Boy, did I feel ridiculous.

"I don't know," I said.

Once, right after my parents' divorce, I flew into a huge rage over an outfit that had ripped. Mom tried to calm me down, but I was so angry, I couldn't see straight. Finally she said, "Close your eyes, take a deep breath, and tell me what you see."

I saw myself in a dry, parched field. My mom and dad were off in the distance, on two high, snow-capped mountains. I knew then what I was really angry about — the split.

I closed my eyes.

This time I was falling through a trapdoor in an airplane, screaming. Looking up through the little black square in the bottom of the plane, I could see Dad at the controls. He was happily fiddling around, having fun, totally oblivious to me.

Tears sprang into my eyes. "I'm sorry, guys," I said. "I think I've been under a lot of pressure."

I felt arms wrapping around me from all sides.

CHAPTER 15

"Hello, everybody," said Ms. Hartley into a mike, "and welcome to Stoneybrook Middle School for the final meet of the Connecticut State Mathletes Championship!"

PHWWEEEEEET! "Wooo! Wooo! Wooo! Wooo!"

This was it. Tuesday night. Full auditorium. And yes, that reaction belonged to Kristy. (Who else?)

She wasn't the only one cheering and whistling. Just the loudest. You'd have thought this was a basketball tournament or a rock concert.

Kristy had arrived early and saved the usual front-row seats for the BSC members and my family. Dad had called to say he might be late, so Kristy had stuffed her coat into his seat to save it.

Did I have stage fright? You bet. All around me, my teammates were talking and waving to friends and brainstorming over problems. I could do nothing but sit and shake. I thought I was having an insulin reaction. I opened my backpack and made sure I had a packet of honey, just in case.

"We are number one!" Jason shouted, right behind my left ear.

I nearly jumped out of my chair.

"Let's have some quiet, please," Ms. Hartley continued. "For those of you who are new to these meets . . ."

As she went on, I tuned out. At the Eastbury table, the entire team was gathered around George Singh. He looked like a boxer surrounded by his trainers and coaches.

"You can do it, Stacey," whispered Emily.

"You're only one point behind him," Bea said.

I felt sick. This was a team meet, not a one-on-one competition. It was selfish to think of the individual scoring record.

But I was.

". . . And so, without further ado, we'll start," Ms. Hartley said. "Eastbury takes the first spin."

The audience fell silent. George Singh spun the wheel.

We were off and running.

When Ms. Hartley read the first question, I could not understand it. Literally. I thought she was speaking in another language. It wasn't until she put it on the overhead projector that I figured out the words.

I don't know how I managed to answer that one correctly. But I did.

And Geoge Singh didn't.

The second one was easy. The third was about repeating numbers (yeaaa!).

Pop. My old self was returning. I was on a roll. I didn't miss a problem until about halfway through.

It wasn't a hard problem. I just happened to look out into the audience while I was figuring it out.

The coat was still on Dad's chair. He hadn't come.

He had lied to me.

The three-minute buzzer went off before I could finish. Luckily, everyone else on my team had answered it right.

Unluckily, so had everyone on the Eastbury team. Including George Singh.

I don't know how I pulled it together after that. Maybe because I refused to look at Dad's seat again. But I did manage to snag all the rest of the questions.

By the end of the meet, the two teams were tied.

"Ladies and gentlemen, this may be the highest scoring meet in Mathletes history!" Ms. Hartley announced. "Before our final team problem, let's give both sides a big hand."

The audience roared.

But the roar was different. I heard something in it I hadn't heard before.

I looked out. Kristy's down coat had transformed into my father.

He was cheering at the top of his lungs, a huge smile on his face.

I smiled back. All my anger flew out the window.

"This is a tricky one." Ms. Hartley put a sequence on the overhead projector. It looked like this:

$$\underline{\Pi} \quad \heartsuit \quad 8 \quad \text{M}$$

"For the final problem of the year, what is the next figure in this sequence? Okay, teams . . . huddle!"

Suddenly I felt eight gusts of breath on my neck.

"Is it code?" Emily asked.

"Another language?" Alexander suggested.

"Maybe if we look at it upside down," Bea said.

I stared and stared. Out of the corner of my eye, I could see George scribbling furiously as his teammates argued.

"Okay, these shapes mean something," I said. "What do they have in common?"

"Nothing," Mari whispered hopelessly.

I began thinking aloud. "Each is one shape, not two . . . four must be enough to determine the fifth . . . they're each symmetrical around a vertical line . . ."

I stared at the symbols. I imagined a vertical line down the center of each.

The answer stared me in the face.

"I've got it!" I screamed.

I picked up the bell and rang it hard.

George Singh slapped his pencil down and groaned.

"St — " Ms. Hartley's voice caught. "Stacey?"

I drew this on a sheet of paper:

"Is this it?" I asked.

Ms. Hartley stared at it. In the hushed auditorium, you could hear her footsteps as she brought the sheet to the overhead projector.

"The four symbols," Ms. Hartley said into the mike, "are a one, a two, a three, and a four — but each is attached to its mirror image." Her face broke into a grin. "And Stacey McGill, by drawing a five the same way, has won *the state championship for Stoneybrook Middle School, and broken the individual state scoring record!*"

She had to shout that last part to be heard over the crowd noise.

Have you ever seen eight Mathletes try to lift another one onto their shoulders? It's hilarious. But somehow they hoisted me up there. At that point, I didn't care if I fell and broke my ankle. I was thrilled.

Kristy was leading a "Two, four, six, eight" cheer. Mom and Dad were rushing onto the stage.

I must have hugged about a hundred people. The last was Dad.

"Congratulations, sweetheart. I am so proud of you," he said.

I felt tears welling up. "Where were you? I didn't think you'd make it."

"Sorry, Stacey. I had to take a taxi from Yonkers. My car broke down on the way."

"Oh, no! It was brand-new!"

Dad shrugged. "I was going to get rid of it. Now that I have a new job, I won't be needing it in the city. Who can afford those outrageous garage rates, anyway?"

Typical.

I smiled, but my mind was busy doing Dad math: New job plus no car equals fewer visits. I could feel a little *clunk* in the pit of my stomach.

"I guess this is good-bye to the New Dad," I said.

Dad laughed. "He was kind of a nuisance, anyway."

"Not to me."

"Don't worry," Dad said softly. "I'm marking lots of Stacey days in my book. And the company has a great arrangement with a rent-a-car place. Maybe the New Dad is gone, but the Old, Improved Dad will be even better."

"Okay."

As we hugged again, I felt someone tugging at my shirttail.

I turned around to see Lindsey. She was holding out a sheet of paper, and she looked ready to explode with excitement. "Stacey, look!"

The page was full of scribbles, but in the middle of it all was a big, smudgy

"That last question — I got it too!" Lindsey blurted out. "I'M JUST AS SMART AS YOU!"

Dad burst out laughing.

So did I. I don't know why, but that was one of the nicest parts of the whole wonderful day.

Dear Reader,

Unlike Stacey and the other kids in the Mathletes, I was never a good math student. Math was difficult for me, I had to work hard at it to get even passing grades, and several times I had to be tutored in order to keep up with my classmates. When I graduated from college, I was thrilled because I thought I would never have to work another math problem again. I was wrong. I find that I use math almost every day, especially when I'm sewing, one of my favorite pastimes. Sewing involves a lot of measuring, figuring, and refiguring. I keep a calculator on my sewing table, and it helps, but there are some things you can only figure out with your brain. So as much as I hated math when I was in school, now I find that I really do need it — and all that hard work paid off.

Happy reading,

Ann M Martin

L. GODWIN

Ann M. Martin

About the Author

ANN MATTHEWS MARTIN was born on August 12, 1955. She grew up in Princeton, NJ, with her parents and her younger sister, Jane.

Although Ann used to be a teacher and then an editor of children's books, she's now a full-time writer. She gets ideas for her books from many different places. Some are based on personal experiences. Others are based on childhood memories and feelings. Many are written about contemporary problems or events.

All of Ann's characters, even the members of the Baby-sitters Club, are made up. (So is Stoneybrook.) But many of her characters are based on real people. Sometimes Ann names her characters after people she knows, other times she chooses names she likes.

In addition to the Baby-sitters Club books, Ann Martin has written many other books for children. Her favorite is *Ten Kids, No Pets* because she loves big families and she loves animals. Her favorite Baby-sitters Club book is *Kristy's Big Day*. (By the way, Kristy is her favorite baby-sitter!)

Ann M. Martin now lives in New York with her cats, Gussie and Woody. Her hobbies are reading, sewing, and needlework — especially making clothes for children.

Notebook Pages

This Baby-sitters Club book belongs to _____.

I am _____ years old and in the _____

grade.

The name of my school is _____.

I got this BSC book from _____.

I started reading it on _____ and

finished reading it on _____.

The place where I read most of this book is _____.

My favorite part was when _____.

If I could change anything in the story, it might be the part when

_____.

My favorite character in the Baby-sitters Club is _____.

The BSC member I am most like is _____

because _____.

If I could write a Baby-sitters Club book it would be about _____

_____.

#105 Stacey the Math Whiz

Stacey's a math whiz — she's even the new state champion!
My favorite subject is ———————————————, because

—————. The biggest math whiz I know is ———————

——————————————. If I were on a —————

team like the Mathletes, these are the people I would want on

my team: —————————————————————

——————————————————————————

——————————————————————. Stacey has a big

dilemma when her father buys her tickets to a rock concert on

the same night as the math championships. If I were Stacey, I

would have chosen to go to —————————————

—————— because —————————————

——————————————. Meanwhile, Claudia learns she's just as

good a math tutor as Stacey when she tutors Lindsey DeWitt.

If I could have one of the BSC members as a tutor, I would

choose ——————————————, because ————

——————————————————————————

—————————————————————————.

STACEY'S

Here I am, age three.

Me with Charlot
my "almost

A family portrait — me
with my parents.

SCRAPBOOK

hanssen,
ster."

Getting ready for school.

In LUV at Shadow Lake.

Illustrations by Angelo Tillery

Read all the books
about **Stacey**
in the Baby-sitters Club series
by Ann M. Martin

Look for #106

CLAUDIA, QUEEN OF THE SEVENTH GRADE

"I have been nominated," I announced, "for — are you ready for this? — Queen of the Seventh Grade. Ta-da!"

"Yeaaaaa!" Mallory cheered.

"Cool," Jessi said.

"You must be joking," Kristy remarked.

"I'm not," I replied. "Joanna and Josh put my name up —"

"Who and who?" Abby asked.

"They're my friends," I explained. "I mean, I know it's ridiculous, but I think it's hilarious."

"Imagine," Stacey said. "Well, even if you were elected, you couldn't accept it."

"Why not?" I asked.

"That would be cheating," Stacey answered.

"You're thirteen, Claudia. Technically, you're an eighth-grader."

"I am? Well, I wasn't allowed to go to the eighth-grade Halloween party. I'm not allowed to eat with the eighth-graders. Officially, I'm as seventh gradish as you can be."

"What kind of time commitment is this . . . Queenship?" Kristy asked.

"Kristyyyy," I said. "This is a *goof*. A *joke*."

"You mean, you weren't really nominated?" Mary Anne asked.

"I was, but I'm not going to win or anything," I answered. "I just think it's funny. Why are you all taking this so seriously?"

Kristy smiled. "For your sake, Claudia. We'd hate for you to actually have to kiss a seventh-grade boy or anything."

"Depends on the boy," Jessi remarked.

"Eeeeew, *Jessi!*" Mallory said.

They both dissolved into giggles.

Rrrrring!

Mary Anne picked up the phone, and we were back to baby-sitting. I didn't bring up the Queen of the Seventh Grade again. No one seemed to think it was as goofy as I did.

Oh, well. It didn't really matter.

I still thought it was nice to be asked.

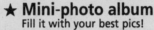
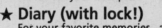